Dangerous Dreams

KidWitness Tales

KiDWiTNESS
T·A·L·E·S

Dangerous Dreams

JIM WARE

BETHANY HOUSE
MINNEAPOLIS, MINNESOTA

A Focus on the Family book
Published by Bethany House Publishers
A Ministry of Bethany Fellowship International
11400 Hampshire Avenue South
Bloomington, Minnesota 55438
www.bethanyhouse.com

Printed in the United States of America by
Bethany Press International, Bloomington, Minnesota 55438

Library of Congress Cataloging-in-Publication Data

Ware, Jim
    Dangerous dreams / by Jim Ware.
       p. cm. — (KidWitness tales)
Summary: Livy, personal slave to Procula, wife of Pontius Pilate, wants her freedom more than anything, but when she encounters Jesus, her ideas of freedom are changed.
    ISBN 1-56179-956-4
    [1. Bible. N.T.—History of Biblical events—Fiction . 2. Jesus Christ—Passion—Fiction. 3. Procula, Claudia—Fiction.] I. Title. II. Series.
    PZ7.W219 Dan   2001
    [Fic]—dc21
                                     00–012433

1 2 3 4 5 6 7 8 9 10 11 12 13 14 15 / 08 07 06 05 04 03 02 01

For Chris and Vicky

JIM WARE is a graduate of Fuller Theological Seminary. He and his wife, Joni, have six kids—Alison, Megan, Bridget, Ian, Brittany, and Callum. Just for fun, Jim plays the guitar and the hammered dulcimer.

CHAPTER 1

Livy stirred and opened her eyes. A copper pot fell from her lap and rolled clanging across the stone-paved floor. It was hot in the palace kitchen, terribly hot. She pushed her sweat-soaked, auburn-red hair out of her face and gulped the dry Palestinian air.

A dream! How long have I been asleep?

She shook herself, then drew a long, slow breath. *Write it down!* she told herself. *Quick! Before it slips away!*

Pulling out the stylus and scrap of parchment tablet that she always kept tucked inside her wide sashlike belt, Livy began to write:

I dreamed again—about Father and Mother and my home back in Gaul. There were snowy mountains and the blue sea and green pines and hillsides covered with wildflowers. Just the way it was almost seven years ago . . . when I was only five. I saw the faces of the people of my village, and . . .

"You there—redhead!" It was the voice of Melanus, Pilate's bald, sharp-nosed Syrian steward. "What do you think you're doing?"

Livy quickly shoved her writing materials back into her belt as Melanus dashed into the kitchen, his arm drawn back to strike her.

"Ow!" she yelled as Melanus cuffed her behind the ear. A noise like the clattering of the pot on the stones rang in her head. A sharp pain shot up her arm and into her shoulder as he seized her by the elbow and dragged her to her feet.

"So! Sleeping at your work again! Scribbling words again! Get up, you stubborn young she-donkey! Do you think Master keeps slaves just so they can lie around dozing and doodling all day? Get back to scrubbing those pots before I take the whip to you!"

"Yes, sir," muttered Livy, wincing at the pain in her arm. She retrieved the pot and sat down heavily on the bench.

"I don't know what possessed Mistress Procula to teach you your letters," said Melanus, glowering down his nose at her. "It was ridiculous—and dangerous! Slaves don't need to know how to read and write. It puts unsafe ideas into their heads. I'm going to be keeping an eye on you!"

Livy said nothing. Instead, she picked up her pumice scrubbing stone and went back to work, making a rude face at Melanus' retreating back as he left the room.

Old Cook came in as the steward went out, followed by young Quintus, the eleven-year-old Greek who was Livy's closest comrade in bondage.

"In trouble *again?*" scolded Cook, wagging her double chin at the pouting girl. "I might have known."

Looking up, Livy saw Quintus shake his bushy head. He shuffled his sandaled feet, crossing and recrossing his bare, birdlike legs as if to show the embarrassment and confusion he felt for his friend. Cook frowned disapprovingly. But when Livy's eyes met hers, the bulky woman's scowl melted into an indulgent smile.

"Oh, what's the use?" said Cook, relaxing her wrinkled forehead and dropping her hands to her sides. "You're just not cut out to be a slave, are you, child?" She sighed. "What happened *this* time?"

"Fell asleep, I guess," the girl answered with a frown. "I was up all night again—talking with Mistress about her dreams. And what's wrong with that? Isn't that why I'm here? I'm supposed to be her personal servant. I'm supposed to take care of her *personal* needs. *That's* why Pilate bought me—not to be a kitchen maid!" She scrunched up her nose in disgust. Her freckled face reddened to match her hair.

"Melanus doesn't see it that way," warned Cook, stepping over to the kitchen fire to stir the kettle. "He says *all* the servants have to take their turns in the kitchen. And he *can* tell you what to do, Missie. So you'd better pay attention. Cross Melanus one too many times, and you'll regret it! You mark my words!"

"Melanus!" spat Livy. "I think he was born to make my life miserable!"

"Hush!" said Cook with a frown.

Livy scowled again, scooped a handful of sand into the pot, gripped the pumice stone, and returned to her scrubbing. Cook shook her head, muttered something to herself, and noisily slooshed a basket of red beans into the boiling water. Then she stepped out into the pantry. Quintus came and sat beside Livy on the bench.

"She's right," he whispered, smoothing down his short and very rumpled tunic. "You're *not* cut out to be a slave. You're always dreaming of bigger things."

Livy glared at him. "No kidding! No Gaul is cut out to be a slave! I have the blood of Celtic chieftains flowing in my veins! Do you know what that means, Quintus?"

Quintus sighed and nodded his scruffy head. "Uh-huh. You told me already. About a hundred times."

She dropped the stone and turned to face him. "Listen! I just had another dream about home. There were pine trees and mountains and wildflowers. And people I used to know when I was very little, all walking around in a place filled with color and light. It was beautiful—almost too beautiful to be real. I don't know if it was

Gaul or the Otherworld . . . that's where my people believe you go after you die."

"Uh-huh," said Quintus, blandly scratching his ear.

"My parents were there, too—which *could* mean that they didn't survive the Roman attack. I wish I knew!" She frowned and bit her lip. "Quintus," she said, looking straight into his eyes. "It's time we got serious!"

Quintus blinked. "About what?"

"About escaping!"

"Come on, Livy." Quintus frowned. "Do you know what the Romans do to runaway slaves?"

"Do *you* know what they did to my village?" The words exploded from her mouth. "To my people? Burned down the houses! Put some to the sword, took the rest away and sold us as slaves! That was almost seven years ago! I still don't know for sure what happened to my parents!" Angry tears filled her eyes.

She was about to say more, but a glance at Quintus' face made it clear that he was no longer listening. His wide, round eyes were fixed on the doorway. His jaw had fallen slack. His face was as white as a sheet of papyrus. His lips were moving wordlessly. She followed his gaze to where a large spotted hound, one of Governor Pilate's household dogs, was trotting over the threshold and across the stone floor toward the steaming stew pot.

Livy's angry tears stopped as suddenly as they had started. The corners of her mouth crept upward in a knowing smile. Quintus' fear of dogs was legendary in the household. Cook's, too. *This could be fun*, Livy thought.

As she watched, Quintus squeezed his eyes tightly shut and let out a piercing yell. "A dog!" he screamed. "A really *big* one! Aaaah!" He jumped up from the bench and burst through the opposite door to the courtyard beyond the kitchen. Just then, Cook stumbled in from the pantry to see what all the ruckus was about.

"*Hoi!*" she screeched, dropping her basket as she caught sight of the drooling animal. Red beans skittered across the floor. "Who let that mangy thing in here? *Chaneni, Adonai!*" Then she fled too, slipping and sliding through the mess of spilled beans in her haste to find the door.

Livy sat back and laughed—a long, luxurious laugh. It felt good. But as she sat there wiping the tears from her eyes, she caught sight of another figure in the doorway— a tall, stately woman in a Roman robe, or *stola*.

"*Domina!*" she exclaimed, jumping to her feet. "What are *you* doing here?"

Procula, the slim and graceful wife of Governor Pontius Pilate, descended the three steps into the kitchen and silently crossed the floor. A warm feeling of affection welled up inside Livy as she looked up at the lady. Procula had been more like a mother than a mistress to the girl ever since the day Pilate had brought Livy home from the auction block in Rome. Livy genuinely loved her mistress. And because she loved her, she couldn't help being troubled by the expression she now saw on her face.

The ringlets of Procula's sandy brown hair, curled in the Roman fashion, could not hide the deep creases in her forehead. There was an odd, distracted look in her brown eyes. Her gracefully arched eyebrows were knit closely together. The shadows under her high cheekbones were darker than usual.

"I've had another dream. Early this morning," she said. "I want to tell you about it. Come."

Taking Livy by the hand, Procula led her out across the courtyard and into the shaded colonnade beyond the palace fountain. There she stopped and made the girl sit beside her on a marble bench.

"What was it this time?" asked Livy, watching her mistress's face with a sense of discomfort. The dark cloud in the lady's eyes made her feel as if the warm April morning had turned suddenly cold. She couldn't remember when she had last seen Procula looking so upset.

The lady turned and faced her. "I'm not exactly sure *what* I saw," she said quietly. "In the beginning, I think it was . . . baskets."

Procula often had troubling dreams. It seemed to Livy that she had been having them even more frequently over the past several weeks. She never told these dreams to anyone but Livy. Procula had recognized Livy's special talent for interpreting dreams from the very beginning. It was part of the girl's Celtic heritage; the Celtic nations—the Gauls, the Britons, the Galatians, the Cymrians, the Milesians—were famous for their emotional temperaments, their mystical leanings, their wild imaginations, and their interest in the unseen world. It was also one of several qualities that had earned her a special place in her mistress's affections—and the keen resentment of Melanus, the steward.

"Baskets," Livy repeated, almost as if she were speaking to herself.

"Yes," said Procula. "Baskets full of fire."

Livy pulled back her long hair, pursed her lips, and half-closed her eyes. She drew her feet up under her and sat cross-legged on the bench, trying to picture the thing in her mind.

"And there was a man," the lady continued. "A man with piercing eyes—eyes that seemed to look straight down into my soul. Standing in front of the Jewish temple. And a lamb."

"A lamb. With the baskets?"

"No—the temple and the lamb came *after* the baskets. At least I think so. What do you think it all means?"

Livy was silent. She hated to admit it, but she was stumped. "Well," she said at last, letting out a slow breath, "maybe it doesn't really mean anything. Not every dream does. Maybe you're just anxious about being in Jerusalem. Master *did* say that he's expecting trouble this year."

Procula sighed. "Yes," she said thoughtfully. "And that *might* explain the part about the temple . . . and the lamb. The Jews *do* sacrifice a lamb at Passover. But what about the rest of it? The man with the piercing eyes? The baskets of fire?"

"I'm not sure," said Livy, shivering involuntarily.

Procula frowned. After a pause she said, "Those eyes keep coming back to me. I can't get them out of my mind! That's why I want you to come with me."

The girl shot her a questioning glance.

"To the temple," Procula explained. "To look for clues. Maybe we'll see something there that will help you. I simply must know what the dream means! If you can tell me, I—well, I'd even be willing to reward you."

"What kind of reward?" Livy asked.

"What kind of reward would you like?"

Livy didn't hesitate. "I want to be set free!"

"Oh, child!" laughed Procula. "For interpreting *one* dream? I don't think so."

Livy's heart sank. Her face fell. Her mistress saw it and hastened to comfort her.

"Of course, I've always thought about setting you free when you've come of age—if you behave yourself. I suppose that's one of the reasons I taught you to read and write."

When I come of age, Livy thought bitterly. *Right! By then I'll probably be too old to care!* Nobody, not even Procula, knew what this meant to Livy. *Nobody*, she thought, *could possibly understand why freedom is so important to me.* Yes, she had a kind, wonderful mistress and a comfortable home. Yes, she was surrounded by good friends like Quintus and Cook. But *freedom* was part of her Celtic heritage too. All the Celts were fiercely independent. They loved liberty! Her father and mother had been slaves to no one! The thought of her parents reminded her how terribly she ached to see them again—even though she knew that wasn't likely to happen after all this time. Still, she'd search the world over for them if only she were free . . .

She glanced up to see her mistress giving her a probing look. "So," said Procula, "will you help me?"

Livy looked into the deep brown eyes of the woman who had been almost like a mother to her for nearly seven years. "Sure," she said quietly. "I'll do what I can."

Procula's face relaxed into a warm smile. "Good. Then you'll accompany me to the temple tomorrow. I'll call for you early—sometime after the morning meal." She rose, took Livy's hand, and squeezed it. Then she turned and walked away.

That was when Livy caught sight of Quintus. He was edging his way carefully down the portico, keeping to the shadows, flitting stealthily from column to column.

"Hey!" he hissed when he caught sight of her. "Is that dog still around?"

Livy laughed. "No, you big coward! But listen!" She ran over to him and gripped him by his bony shoulders. "Tomorrow Mistress is taking me with her to the Jewish temple. And I want *you* to come along!"

"Me? What for?"

"Don't you know anything?" she said. "It's Passover week! The place will be simply crawling with hordes of people!"

"So what?"

"*So what?*" Livy pressed her nose to his and lowered her voice. "It will be the perfect time and place to make our escape. *That's* what!"

CHAPTER 2

L ivy! Look!"

She was plotting out possible escape routes when Quintus' voice broke in upon her thoughts. They were standing with the lady Procula at the top of a wide ramp, beneath a lofty pillared archway. Within lay the first of the temple's outer courts, the Court of the Gentiles—a large paved plaza teeming with men, women, and children from every part of the known world. Quintus touched her arm and let out a low whistle.

The people in the court were as different as the various countries from which they had come. There were dark-eyed Jews from Egypt, fat, oily merchants from Parthia, exotic black Ethiopians, olive-skinned Greeks and Syrians, a few fair-haired Galatians (who made Livy feel at home), toga-clad Roman officials, soldiers in bright armor, and lots of native Jerusalemites. Most of the Jewish men had covered their heads with the traditional blue-and-white prayer shawl. Around their forearms and heads were bound long, snaky leather straps to which were attached tiny scripture boxes, or *phylacteries*. The air was filled with the bleating of sheep and goats, the calls of the moneychangers, the hum of voices, and the fragrance of roasting meat—the result of the almost continual animal sacrifices.

Livy sighed as she looked out over this multicolored sea of people. Would she see anything here that might help her grasp the meaning of her mistress's dream? And what if she *did* interpret it correctly? Procula's promise to free her when she "came of age" meant at least eight or nine more years of slavery. *Eight or nine years!* She made a face and shook her head. *It might as well be forever!* It wasn't a very encouraging picture. How much easier to get lost in the crowd and make a quick break for it!

A trumpet sounded in the distance—the ritual *shofar,* or ram's horn. At the noise, everyone turned toward the sanctuary, the house of the Jewish God—a massive structure of square blocks and towers that overshadowed the entire temple area.

"This way!" said Procula, motioning to them to follow her. Carefully they threaded their way through the multitude of worshipers and visitors.

Livy craned her neck and stared. The sight of the temple itself nearly took her breath away. To her it looked like a fairy palace, all shining and golden in the morning sun. She recalled a snatch of verse she'd once heard Cook recite:

> *Far off appearing like a Mount of alabaster,*
> *Topped with golden spires . . .*

Soon they stood before a low wall of marble, intricately ornamented with carvings of grapevines and pomegranates. Beyond it stood the entrance to the first of the temple's *inner* courts—the Court of the Women. Upon this wall was a stone tablet, and on the tablet was inscribed a message in Latin and Greek:

> *No foreigner may pass this barrier.*
> *Anyone caught doing so*
> *Will be responsible for his own ensuing death.*

"Does that mean *us*?" asked Livy, scrunching up her freckled nose.

"Yes," said Procula, unveiling her face just long enough to give the girl a warning look.

"You mean they'd actually *kill* us? Just for going past this little wall?"

"They would."

"I don't believe it!"

Quintus rolled his eyes. "Believe it, Livy," he said.

Hmph! thought Livy. *How am I supposed to find any clues if I can't even get inside?*

Suddenly she had an inspiration. Elbowing Quintus

in the ribs, she whispered, "You stay here. And keep watching for a good chance to get away. I'm going to see what I can find out about *Domina*'s dream."

Quintus blinked and stared. "Okay," he said.

Eluding her mistress's watchful eye, Livy ran straight up to the guard who kept the entrance to the Court of the Women. He was a large, thick-lipped, burly man, who wore the brass helmet, white turban, and blue tunic of the temple guards. In his right hand he held a long iron-tipped spear, in his left a polished round shield. Livy stood in front of him and uncovered her head.

"Excuse me, sir," she said in a loud, official-sounding voice. "I represent the governor's wife."

A dark man in a gray hooded cloak who stood nearby gave a short laugh. "That's a good one!" he observed, stroking the head of a big black dog that sat patiently at his feet.

Livy ignored the dark man's comment and kept her attention fixed upon the guard. He lowered his brassy shield and stared straight into her eyes. It was clear that he had never seen anyone quite like the tall, blue-eyed, freckle-faced, copper-haired girl. "What are you?" he said at last, curling his lip and raising his bushy brows.

"Not *what*," she said. "*Who*. And I told you. Servant to Procula, wife of Pontius Pilate. My mistress—" she jerked a thumb in the lady's direction, "—would like to have a look around inside."

The man in the gray cloak raised his dark eyebrows. Livy glared at him.

The guard's face turned very red. "Gentiles," he said, "are *forbidden* to enter."

Livy wasn't about to give up. "Don't you get it? I'm not talking about just *any* Gentile. This is the wife of *Caesar's representative* in Jerusalem!"

"Huh!" grunted the guard. "Caesar *himself* would not be permitted to pass!" He straddled the opening in the barrier, holding his spear diagonally across the space. "Now go away!"

Livy scowled. *Regroup. Rethink.* She bent her head, wrinkled up her nose, and pressed the palm of her left hand against her forehead.

"Oh, no!" she said after a moment's silence, looking up suddenly as if distracted by a noise. She pointed urgently to the shaded portico across the courtyard where the tables of the moneychangers had been set up. "Over there! Is that a robbery? I'm almost *sure* it's a robbery!"

The guard bent down and sneered in her face. "Sorry," he said. "Your tricks won't work here. Now go!"

Maybe if I make him really *mad.* "All right," she said, edging away. "I'll go. But I'm going to tell Governor Pilate about you."

"Ha!" laughed the man. "And just what are you going to tell him?"

"That you've got a nose like a *pig*—that's what!" She flattened her own nose with the tip of her thumb and stuck out her tongue. Then she turned and ran. The dark man in the gray cloak burst out laughing.

"Why, you little—!" spluttered the guard, gripping his spear with white-knuckled hands. "When I catch you, I'll—I'll—" He took off after her with fire in his eyes.

Livy darted between a lanky, bearded worshiper in a prayer shawl and a gray-headed woman carrying two pigeons in a small wooden cage. The guard, in hot pursuit, tripped over the woman, knocking her cage to the ground and freeing the birds. They soared into the sky alongside the guard's curses.

Livy chuckled and dodged back toward the entrance to the Court of the Women. Then, covering her red hair with her cloak, she dashed past the forbidden barrier, across a paved esplanade, and up the steps to the magnificent Nicanor Gate. Here she stopped, panting and breathless. *Did anyone see me?* she wondered. She glanced nervously to one side, then the other, thinking all the while of the words inscribed on the tablet: *Anyone caught doing so will be responsible for his own ensuing death.* Deciding that the coast was clear, Livy turned her attention to the Court of the Israelites, and beyond that to the Court of the Priests and the sanctuary itself, searching for something—anything—that might help her understand the meaning of Procula's dream. She wasn't prepared for what she found.

Near the door of the sanctuary, atop a massive stone pedestal mounted by a wide ramp, rose a high, four-horned altar of rough-hewn stones. Beside the altar stood a bearded priest dressed in white. A large knife glittered in his right hand. His left hand rested upon the head of a lamb that lay stretched upon the altar. As the priest raised the knife, the lamb turned its head and looked directly at Livy. It was strange, but even at that distance she could see the animal's face clearly—a sad, silent, suffering face. Suddenly she let out a gasp.

"Oh!" she said. "The eyes!"

How could it be? To Livy, the lamb's eyes looked exactly like *human* eyes. The eyes of a man. Deep, piercing eyes. Eyes that seemed to be looking straight into her soul.

She lifted her hand to her mouth and gave a stifled cry. The knife fell. She turned and ran.

Livy burst out into the Court of the Gentiles only to find the whole place in an uproar. People were rushing in every direction, knocking one another down, tripping over each other, shoving each other aside. From the portico of the moneychangers came the voices of men raised in angry protest. Livy heard shouts, the crunch of shattering wood, and several loud cracking sounds.

Looking up, she saw a man—a tall, strong man in a peasant's tunic—swinging a whip made of leather

thongs, tipping over the tables of the merchants and bro-
kers, freeing the sacrificial animals that were for sale.
Doves and pigeons went fluttering into the faces of be-
fuddled onlookers. Young lambs sported and played
through the crowd. Goats ran this way and that. Children laughed and cried. Men yelled at the tops of their
voices.

All at once it hit her. *This is it!* she thought. *The perfect chance to make a run for it!* But first she'd have to
find Quintus. Frantically she surveyed the chaotic scene
for some sign of the skinny boy with the wild hair. At
last she saw him emerging from behind a man with a pair
of goats on a tether.

"Come on!" she shouted. "Let's go! It's now or
never!"

But Quintus wasn't listening. Once again his face had
gone pale and his brown eyes were wide with terror. Livy
saw him open his mouth in a scream. "A dog!" he yelled.
"A dog! A big black dog!"

Not now! she thought.

In the next instant a flash of black fur bounded past
her, closely followed by the dark man in the gray hood
and cloak. The dog leaped up at poor Quintus, knocking
him to the ground and licking his face.

The man in the gray cloak charged up and pulled the
animal off the boy. Then, without a word of apology or
explanation, he hurried off through the crowd with his

dog. When he had gone, Livy dashed over to Quintus and helped him to his feet.

In the next instant she felt a hand on her arm. She turned to see Procula standing beside her.

"It's all right, *Domina*," said the girl, her heart sinking at the thought of the lost opportunity. "He's shaken, but I don't think he's hurt."

But a glance told her that Procula wasn't thinking about Quintus or the dog at all. Instead, she was pointing urgently at the scene in the colonnade.

"That man!" she said breathlessly. "The one with the whip! I think it's *him!* The one I saw in my dream!"

CHAPTER 3

Drove them all out," said old Hatshup, grinning and bobbing his grizzled head. "Sent them packing, he did! Every last one of them. They say you could hear those moneychangers howling and whining all the way across the Hinnom Valley!"

Livy looked up from the flat, round loaf of bread at which she had been halfheartedly nibbling. Somehow she didn't seem to have much appetite this morning. She'd missed the perfect chance to escape—all because of Quintus and his fear of dogs! And her experience in the temple had left her feeling a bit dazed. *Was it just another dream?* She'd had to ask herself that question several times since awakening that morning. It was too much to think about, too much to take in. She chewed the dry bread and swallowed hard.

"He's an extraordinary man, this Jesus of Nazareth," Hatshup was observing. "I don't care what the priests say about him."

From her place in the corner near the charcoal brazier Livy stared across the smoky kitchen at the gray-haired Egyptian gardener. He was squatting on the stone floor beside the big clay oven, slurping hot broth from a wooden spoon. She saw him shake his head and smack his lips to emphasize the seriousness of his speech. That was when she realized what the old man was talking about. The scene in the temple. The man with the whip of thongs—the one Procula said she had seen in her dream. Livy listened with greater interest.

"He's a good deal more than an extraordinary man if you ask me!" said Cook, turning from the big kettle and shaking her ladle at the old man. Her sleeves were rolled up for work and her flabby upper arms jiggled in time with the flapping of her double chin as she gave her head a vigorous nod. "Some think he might be the Messiah!"

Livy laid her bread aside. "What's the Messiah?" she wanted to know.

No one responded. Instead, bald Melanus put down his bowl, wiped his chin, and rose from the table. *"Some?"* he sneered. "Like that rabble that followed him into the city on Sunday, for instance? Ignorant peasants! Waving their palm branches and singing songs about the 'Son of David.' Honestly!" He gave Cook a condescending smile. "My dear woman, do we really need any more messiahs? What's the count so far this year?"

"Well, there's the one who caused all that trouble up

in Galilee last fall," volunteered Hatshup. "Leader of the zealots. What do they call him?"

"Bar Abbas," snorted Cook. "Fine messiah he'd make!"

"What are *zealots?*" asked Livy.

"Freedom fighters," said Hatshup through a mouthful of broth. "The kind who would like to see Master Pilate and the rest of the Romans on the end of a skewer!" He smiled and nodded, then rose shakily to his feet and handed his bowl to Cook for a second helping.

Freedom fighters! thought Livy. She pulled her piece of parchment from her belt and made herself a note: *Bar Abbas. Freedom fighters. Find out more.*

Looking up, she noticed Quintus, who sat beside her munching his own breakfast, watching her intently out of narrowed eyes. "What are you writing?" he asked.

Livy made a face at him and said nothing.

"Yes, indeed!" laughed Melanus as he started toward the door. "I'd say old Bar Abbas has got more muscle in his arm than this fellow from Nazareth. Perhaps *he's* your messiah after all!"

That word again.

Cook stopped stirring. She dropped the ladle into its rest and wiped her hands on her apron. Then she turned a withering glance on the retreating steward. "You mark my words, Melanus," she said, shaking a finger at him. "The real Messiah—when he comes—won't be a thing like that Bar Abbas. Not a thing like him!"

Livy was becoming exasperated. "What are you talking about? What's a *messiah*, anyway?"

Cook turned and looked at her. "The Deliverer," she said with an earnestness in her voice that nearly took the girl's breath away. "The Liberator. The True King. The One who will set us *all* free."

"And long may he reign!" said Melanus with cheerful sarcasm. "But just remember: Anyone who goes around talking about a king other than Caesar—or whose quest for freedom leads him to challenge the authorities—and I do mean *anyone*," he added, glancing around the room, "will be severely dealt with. *Severely*. Rebels must not be tolerated. That's Master's view, and I share it." He stepped out into the passage. "Now! To work, all of you. The day's wasting!" He strolled off, the back of his bald head reflecting the dim light as he went. Old Hatshup tottered after him, smiling and muttering.

Livy pursed her lips, bowed her head, and wrote again: *Messiah. Liberator. King.*

What if it's true? she thought, biting the end of the stylus. *Would he set* me *free?*

"Now then—no dawdling, you two!" Livy started violently and shoved the parchment and stylus into her sash. Cook was standing over her, waving a thick finger in her face and pulling Quintus up from the bench by the collar of his tunic. "I've put on a stew for the midday meal," Cook continued, "but I need more water and fire-wood. Hurry up now, or I'll send old Melanus after you with a big stick!"

Quintus got up and grabbed a water jar. "I'm going!" he said.

"You too, Missie," said Cook, taking Livy by the arm and hauling her up from her seat. The piece of parchment fell to the floor beside the brazier as the big woman shoved her toward the courtyard door. "Out to the fuel bin with you. And mind you keep that door shut—the courtyard gate, too. I've seen one of those street dogs nosing around out there—a big black one—and I don't want him anywhere near my stew!"

"A big black dog?" said Quintus, turning pale. He clutched the water jar to his chest and hurried out to the fountain.

Livy stood at the door, chuckling as she watched him go. Suddenly an idea struck her. *Perfect!* she thought.

She walked out into the courtyard and glanced quickly around. No one. Even the guard had stepped away from his post for a moment. Livy ran to the gate. Sure enough, there was the dog—a big, snuffling, woolly black thing—a lot like the dog that had jumped all over Quintus at the temple. Slowly and soundlessly she un-latched the gate and pushed it open. Then she hurried to the fuel bin, grabbed an armload of grape wood, and carried it into the kitchen, making sure to leave the door just slightly ajar.

"Here's the fuel, Cook," she said, trying hard not to smile.

"Over there," said Cook, waving a bouncing arm at the opposite wall. "Now you just keep stirring this," she added, handing the ladle to Livy, "while I—"

The door flew open. A black blur exploded into the kitchen. Cook lifted up her voice and screamed. Then she picked up the skirts of her tunic and hurried out the door as the dog knocked over a table, scattered a bowl of shelled lentils across the floor, and bounded over to the stew pot.

Livy laughed and dipped a ladleful of stew into a bowl for the hungry animal. "Good boy!" she said. "You were *great!* Right on time, too!"

The dog barked happily, wagged his tail, and began slurping up the broth. Livy leaned against the wall, watching him eat and laughing to herself. *Who would've thought a woman that size could run so fast?* she thought. *I wish it had been Melanus!* She stroked the dog's head and filled the bowl a second time. "But Quintus is the one I *really* wanted you to meet. I wonder what's taking him so long?"

She reached for the door and yanked it open. "Quintus! Where are you?" she called. "Quintus—!" But the boy's name stuck in her throat.

She stared. She caught her breath.

There in the doorway stood the dark man in the gray hooded cloak—the same man she remembered seeing at the temple the day before.

He smiled at her from behind a thick black beard. "Good morning," he said. "I believe you have my dog."

CHAPTER 4

Who are you?" demanded Livy, backing into the kitchen as the man pushed his way inside. "What are you doing here?"

"I came to talk to *you*," he said. Firmly but noiselessly he shut the door behind him. Then he threw back his hood, revealing a round, close-cropped head and muscular neck. His eyes were as black as his beard and hair. A ragged scar stretched from the middle of his forehead to his left temple. The top half of his left ear was missing.

"Me?" Livy eyed him carefully. "Why in the world do you want to talk to *me*?" He looked dangerous, she thought, and yet she didn't feel afraid of him in the least—only curious. The scar, the wounded ear, the tough, sinewy neck and arms—they were the marks of a fighter.

The visitor, unruffled by her boldness, advanced slowly into the room. As he did so, the big dog trotted over to him, wagging its tail and licking his hand.

"Good dog, Kalb," said the man, gently stroking the animal's head. "I sent him to follow you," he explained, looking up at Livy. "I've come to make you an offer—an offer I believe you will find most interesting."

She shook the hair out of her face. "That's ridiculous!" she laughed scornfully. "You don't even know me!"

Livy was warming to her role in this interesting little drama. It was fun to swagger and put on a brave front. What's more, she found this intruder fascinating. Never had she met anyone like him since the day the Romans captured her and took her away from her home in Gaul. He was completely unlike the grown-up Romans she'd been living with for the last six years. Except for her mistress, who liked to talk about dreams and seemed to have a strong interest in invisible things like the Otherworld, *they* were all very predictable and proper and boring. This man, on the other hand, struck her as being wild and free. He was shrouded in an air of adventure and mystery. And though he was obviously a Jew, there were qualities about him she had never seen in any Jewish man before: a fierce passion, an intense fire in the eyes. As she looked at him, a shadowy picture of her father took shape in her mind's eye—the bold, defiant Celtic warrior-chief, the man who carries the scars of many battles and bows his knee to no one.

"You're right, of course," he said with a cool stare. "I *don't* know you—yet. But I do know something *about* you. Enough, anyway. I know, for instance, that you're a slave . . . personal servant to the governor's wife. You said so yourself—yesterday, in the Court of the Gentiles. I saw what you did there, too. Very bold. Very resourceful. 'The girl has spirit,' I said to myself. That's why I sent Kalb after you. That's why I determined to look you up." He paused and regarded her curiously. "You don't like being a slave, do you?"

Livy scowled and stuck out her lower lip. "Would *you?*"

The smile suddenly faded from the bearded lips. "No. I *don't!*" he said fiercely. "And I *won't* go on being a slave to the Romans—not without a fight. For years I've dreamed of throwing off the yoke of their oppressive rule—of being free! That's why I'm here. I need your help."

"*My* help?"

"I know I'm taking a big risk. But after seeing you in action yesterday, I'm convinced it's worth it. I'm fighting to free my people from slavery to Rome. And I believe you can help me."

Freedom fighters. Zealots, she thought. *So that's it! He's one of them.*

With that, a tiny flame began to burn in that spot just beneath her heart where she always had her strongest feelings. So he was fighting for freedom! And it was clear that he wanted it badly enough to die for it, and that he wanted it *now*—not eight or 10 years from now. He looked like the kind of man who could fight and win, too—the kind of man she and Quintus would *have* to have on their side if their own quest for freedom were ever to succeed.

"But how can *I* help *you?*" she asked. "What do you want from me?"

His eyes narrowed. His voice was low and intense. "I need someone inside the governor's household—someone with ears to hear and eyes to see. I need to know how much the Romans know . . . what they're thinking, what they're planning. Inside information."

"A *spy,* you mean?" asked Livy.

As she waited for his answer, it struck her that he was no longer looking at her face, but rather at her feet. *No,* not her feet—something on the floor *next* to her feet! She allowed her own gaze to drop. Then she saw it.

The parchment! There it lay, face up on the paving stones, the words on its surface plain for anyone to see.

Before she could think or make a move the man in the dark cloak had lunged forward. He seized the parchment, came up with it in his hand, and stood reading it, a slow smile spreading over his bearded face.

"Well!" he said warmly. "What have we here? *Bar Abbas . . . Freedom fighters . . . Messiah . . . Liber-*

ator... King... Find out more. Looks like somebody's a step ahead of me! Somebody around here is speaking my language! Did *you* write this?"

Livy's palms were sweating. Her heart was pounding so hard that she thought the man must surely be able to hear it. She scrunched up her nose and scowled at him. "What if I did?" she shot back.

"Well, for one thing, it could be very uncomfortable for you if this were to fall into the wrong hands. *Very* uncomfortable."

"Like *your* hands, for instance?"

His dark eyebrows lifted. "What do *you* think?"

"How do I know what to think? Why should I trust you or believe anything you say?"

He smiled. "It looks like you haven't any choice... now that I've got *this*," he said, holding up the parchment. "But I think there's an even better reason. I think you share my dream—the dream of freedom. It's a dangerous dream, true. But you believe that the danger's worth it. Am I right?"

Livy said nothing. Her heart was burning within her. Through her imagination raced the images she had seen in her dream of home. Her mother's face. Her father's flashing sword. The sea and the coastline of Gaul. The pink, purple, and yellow flowers. The faces of old friends and neighbors. She wanted it all so badly that she could taste it.

"Think of it!" the dark man was saying. "If my friends and I succeed, you'll be free to go anywhere you want to go!"

Footsteps outside. *Oh, no!* she thought. *Cook's coming back!*

The man threw himself against the door and held it shut. Someone on the other side began to knock.

Livy felt her stomach knotting. What would happen to her if she were caught talking to a freedom fighter? If he were forced to hand over her writing tablet? If she were discovered plotting revolution, planning escape? She glanced at her visitor. He gave her a grim look.

"C'mon, Livy!" called a small voice from the other side of the door. "No more jokes, okay?"

She breathed a sigh of relief. *Quintus!*

The stranger searched her face. "Hold the door," he whispered, "while I find a place to hide! And don't forget," he hissed, holding up the piece of parchment, "I've still got *this!*"

Livy laughed. "It's just Quintus." She cast a glance at Kalb and smiled to herself. "Go ahead and open the door."

The stranger studied her closely.

"Go on," she said. "It's all right."

Without a word, he eased the door open a crack. Quintus shoved his way inside, water jar first. "Took you long enough!" he said.

As the door closed behind him, the boy stopped and stared. Resisting an urge to laugh, Livy followed his eyes to the dark, furry shape in the corner. She saw the color drain away from his face. She saw his eyes and mouth pop wide open.

"The dog!" he cried. "The big black dog! Aaahhh!"

Livy saw Quintus' eyeballs roll up into his head as the huge animal, its tail wagging happily, sprang upon him. The dog planted its paws on the boy's shoulders and began licking his face. Quintus tottered. He swayed. He fell. The water jar crashed to the floor, spilling its contents across the paving stones.

The man in the gray cloak glanced over at Livy, his eyebrows raised toward the ceiling.

"Don't worry," she said, smiling. "He's on *our* side."

CHAPTER 5

O n Wednesday morning, Livy's mistress woke her while the sky outside the window was just beginning to tremble with a pinkish glow. She rubbed her eyes, brushed the red hair out of her face, and sat staring absently as the lady explained her reasons for coming so early.

Procula had dreamed again—the same disturbing dream. As a result, she was determined to see the man called Jesus once more. She wanted to speak to him if possible, to listen to his words. And she had heard that he was teaching in the temple every day. It was decided that Livy and Quintus would accompany her to the Court of the Gentiles that very afternoon.

This, Livy thought, would be a perfect chance to confer with the dark man in the gray cloak. At their parting on the previous day, they had agreed to communicate with each other at every possible opportunity. And so when Kalb showed up in the street that morning, according to plan—it was understood that the dog signaled his master's presence in the neighborhood—Livy slipped out of the courtyard, found the zealot standing under a shadowed archway just outside the gate, and quickly arranged to meet him at the temple that afternoon.

The zealot. That was what she called him. She didn't know his real name. When she asked him for it, he merely smiled, winked, and said, "I am the son of my father. What else do you need to know about me?"

By the time they reached the temple grounds, the sun was angling down over the Hinnom Valley to the west. The air was still very hot. Except for the absence of the whip and the moneychangers' shouts, the scene was almost as hectic as it had been on Monday. If anything, the number of visitors and worshipers in the plaza had increased. The lively festival atmosphere was even more pronounced. Everywhere were the bleats of goats and sheep and the fluttering and cooing of doves and pigeons. The blue smoke of burning sacrifices hung in the air above the enclosure.

"Over there!" said Livy suddenly, tugging at her mistress's sleeve and pointing to a shady spot under the portico. She was proud of herself for having spotted him. Jesus was seated in the middle of a large crowd of people, speaking to them in a clear, strong voice.

"Come," said Procula, pulling the edge of her short

cloak, or *pallium,* up over her head and taking Livy by the hand. Together they moved toward the knot of people for a closer look. Quintus followed at a safe distance.

As they neared the edge of the audience it became increasingly difficult to see the speaker's face. Livy clung to Procula's arm, bobbing her head from side to side, standing on her toes, and ducking this way and that in an attempt to gain a clearer view. Quintus, she noticed, was doing the same. Catching his attention, she mouthed the words, "Keep an eye out for *you-know-who.*" Quintus nodded and went back to the work of seeking a glimpse of Jesus' face.

"Anyone who sins becomes a slave of sin," the voice of Jesus was saying. "So stop sinning! Let the Son set you free. That's the way to be *really* free!"

Slave. Free. Really free! Could it be that Cook was right about this man? Livy wondered. Had he really come to free the slaves? She had to admit that his stunt with the whip was pretty bold and daring. She decided to listen more closely.

"What's he talking about?" mumbled a portly man in a blue-and-white prayer shawl who was standing at her elbow. "Just who is this 'son,' anyway?"

"I think he means himself," responded a slight, plain-faced young woman beside him—apparently his daughter.

Livy, who was still holding on to Procula's arm, felt

her mistress tremble. She looked up and saw that the lady's eyes were fixed intently upon the speaker. An indescribable light was glowing in her face. Livy saw it and shivered.

"*Himself!* Well, no wonder then!" scoffed the man in the prayer shawl, puffing out his cheeks and blowing.

"No wonder what?" asked the Lady Procula, turning suddenly.

"No wonder the priests and the Pharisees are so anxious to see him locked up—that's what!" he answered. "They aren't a bit pleased with *him,* I can tell you!"

Now Livy's curiosity was stirred. There might be something to a man who could inspire that kind of fear in the hearts of the rulers. *Deliverer. Liberator. The True King. Messiah.* Somehow she *had* to get a better look at this Jesus. Leaning heavily on Procula's shoulder, she raised herself to the very tips of her toes, craned her neck, and strained to see over the heads of the people in front of her.

The first thing she saw was his eyes. Livy held her breath. Was it possible? They were like the eyes she had seen in the face of the lamb on the altar—eyes incredibly deep and full of human feeling . . . more feelings than she could name. They held sorrow and pain, but also a deep quietness and a strange kind of joy. Now she understood why those eyes had so haunted her mistress. Now she knew why Procula was so driven to seek out the man who possessed them.

As for the human face in which those eyes were set—well, it was rather disappointing, she thought. In every other detail it was an unimpressive face. A normal face. Definitely *not* the face of a fighter or a liberating king.

"Come to Me," the voice was saying, "if you're tired, worn out, and weighed down. I will give you rest. *I* will give you peace. Get under the yoke with *Me*. Follow *My* example. I am gentle and humble."

Gentle. Yes! *Humble*. That was it! That, she thought, was the whole problem in a nutshell! Livy could not imagine any chieftain back in Gaul boasting about being gentle or humble! She could not picture any Celtic warrior with a face like this man's face. It bore no battle scars. It showed no trace of the fierce pride she remembered seeing in her father's face the last time he rode out to do battle with the Roman legions. It was, indeed, a *gentle* face, a *humble* face—the face of a common peasant. How could a man with such a face set *anybody* free? Livy scrunched up her nose and dropped back down on her heels. She had seen enough.

A tug at her sleeve shook her out of this stream of thought.

"Livy! Look! Over there! It's him!"

She turned. Quintus was pointing to a dark corner behind two huge pillars about fifty paces from the edge of the crowd. Sure enough. It was the zealot, his bearded face half hidden in the shadow of his gray hood, his great black dog panting patiently at his side.

Livy glanced up at Procula. It was obvious that the lady was aware of nothing but the teacher's voice. *Looks like the coast is clear*, she thought. She grasped Quintus by the shoulders and shoved him in the direction of the dark man. "Let's go," she whispered. "We've got an appointment to keep!"

Quintus, whose eyes were riveted on the black shape hunched at the man's side, shook his head until his hair stood out like a ball of freshly washed lamb's wool. He raised a skinny arm and waved her on. "You go ahead," he said.

"Come *on!* He won't bite."

"Which one? The dog or the man?"

Livy glared at him. "Neither one. But *I* will if you don't follow me right *now!*"

Why does he have to be so exasperating? she wondered as they crossed the pavement. She had an extra-special reason for being frustrated with Quintus' reluctance. As of early that afternoon, they actually had something to tell the man in the dark cloak: an important bit of information that Quintus had overheard while serving at Pilate's table during the midday meal. Livy smiled to herself. This business of spying might be dangerous—she knew only too well how dangerous. But it was fun, too.

The zealot flashed his teeth at them from behind black whiskers as they approached. He beckoned to Livy with his hand. "What have you heard?"

"Tell him, Quintus!" she said.

But Quintus hung back, eyeing the dog uncomfortably. "If you'll promise to hold onto that dog," he said, frowning.

The zealot smiled again. "Don't worry, my young friend," he said. "I've got him firmly in hand. He won't hurt you."

Quintus sauntered into the shaded corner and wiped his nose with his sleeve. "Well . . ." he drawled, "Master Pilate got a message from Herod Antipas last night."

The zealot tightened his lips and squeezed his eyebrows together in a dark knot. "And?"

"Antipas told Pilate to be on the lookout for two men—this Jesus—" he pointed in the direction of the Galilean teacher, "—and somebody else named Bar Abbas. He's expected to show up in Jerusalem soon. Maybe this week."

"Do you know him?" asked Livy. "Is he a friend of yours?"

"Possibly." The man lowered his eyes within the shadow of his hood and chewed the fringe of his beard. "And what's Pilate thinking? What's his strategy?"

Quintus spoke up. "Well, when I was serving at the table I heard him say that he wants more soldiers in Jerusalem."

"Sounds like he's expecting trouble," Livy observed.

"More soldiers," repeated the zealot meditatively, fingering the handle of a sword that he wore concealed beneath his cloak. "That's bad. Very bad. We may lose our chance if we wait any longer."

"Lose our chance?" asked Livy.

"Yes. Perhaps the time for action has arrived." He turned and laid a hand on her shoulder. "Thank you, my bold young friends. I am grateful for your help. And I *will* make it up to you—provided, of course," and here he reached into his cloak and pulled out the parchment tablet, "that we maintain the terms of our agreement."

Livy nodded and said nothing.

"Stay true to me and I won't betray you. And be ready for anything. If nothing changes, look for Kalb outside your gate about this time tomorrow. When you see *him*, you'll know *I'm* not far away. Until then, see what else you can find out. *Shalom!*"

He held up his hand in a gesture of farewell. The next moment he and the dog had disappeared into the crowd.

CHAPTER 6

"A silver *drachma* for your thoughts, *Domina*," said Livy that night as she poured water from a glossy black Greek urn into an ornate porcelain basin.

Procula was kneeling before the basin on an intricately embroidered Persian cushion. The room around her was richly appointed with every imaginable comfort and luxury: thick patterned rugs from Arabia, tapestries and wall hangings from India, shiny Parthian brass lamps spouting bright tongues of yellow flame, a couch spread with the finest Egyptian linen. The scent of perfumed lamp oil filled the air. Through the lacelike gratings over the windows a strange, restless sound drifted up from the streets of Jerusalem.

The lady loosened the flowing sleeves of her robe, leaned her head back, and waited for Livy to tie up her sandy brown curls. The tension in her face relaxed into a smile. "You don't have a silver *drachma*," she laughed.

"Well, if I did, I'd give it to know what's on your

mind," said Livy. "You've been awfully quiet since we got back from the temple this afternoon."

Procula sighed. "You're right, of course. But then it's not every day that you hear such words . . . or look into the eyes of a man and come away feeling that . . . well, that you've been changed somehow."

Livy scrunched up her nose. "Are you talking about Jesus?"

The lady turned to face her. "What did you think of him?"

"Me? That he had a nice voice, I guess. I didn't really understand what he was talking about, though. How can you be humble and gentle and still set slaves free? Besides, he wasn't exactly what I pictured when I heard Cook talking about a messiah and deliverer and king."

Not much of a king at all, she added to herself as she held the soft mass of hair between her hands. As her fingers touched her mistress's curls, a picture of the dark man in the gray cloak appeared before her mind's eye. The muscular neck, the scarred face, the protruding jaw. *Now* that's *a man who could beat the Romans if he tried*, she thought. She saw him standing in the shadows, his hand fingering the hilt of his sword. And she thought about the plot into which she had entered with him . . . and of what might happen to Pilate and Procula if it succeeded. Tenderly, she secured the fragrant hair with a gilded ivory comb.

"But you *will* admit," said the lady, turning her head again, "that there is something remarkable about him." She paused a moment, then said, "Did you notice his eyes?"

Wait! thought Livy. *Yes! The eyes! The dream! The lamb on the altar!* She *knew* she had been trying to remember something! Why hadn't she realized it before?

She knelt on the cushion beside Procula and peered intently into her face. "*Domina*—I never told you what I saw on Monday . . . in the temple."

Procula returned her look. "No—you didn't. And *I* never told you the rest of my dream. We both had too much on our minds, I suppose."

"There was *more* to your dream?"

"Yes. And I'm beginning to believe more firmly than ever that it all has something to do with *God* . . . and with my desire to know more about Him. It's got something to do with Jesus, too. He *is* the man I saw in the dream—the man with the piercing eyes! There is so much that I do not understand . . ." Her voice trailed off.

"Go on," pressed Livy. "What else did you see in the dream? Tell me."

"Well," the lady continued, "I don't think I mentioned that the baskets I saw—the baskets filled with fire—were absolutely *huge*—as big as houses. Or that someone was walking among the flames . . ." She faltered, staring at her own reflection in the bowl of water.

Suddenly Livy clutched her mistress's arm. "Just a minute!" she said. "Huge baskets? On fire? With someone inside?" *It can't be!* she thought. It was too horrible to think about . . . and yet the picture was familiar. It was something out of her childhood in Gaul. "I know what it is!"

Procula turned to her. "Then tell me!" she said. "Somehow I feel that it is *extremely* important!"

Livy swallowed. "It's a sacrifice!"

"A sacrifice!"

"Yes! It's the way they make sacrifices to their gods back home in Gaul." She shivered just thinking about it. "Those weren't baskets you saw, *Domina,*" she continued in a moment. "They were *cages*—big cages made of wattle, or wickerwork. The Gauls put people inside those cages and set them on fire!"

"People?" gasped Procula. "I have heard of such things, but I didn't dare believe it!"

"Sometimes—not always—the victims go willingly . . . for the good of the tribe. You know—to save failing crops or get rid of a plague or something like that. And the Gauls believe that when they *do* go willingly, they pass into the Otherworld after death—a place of light and beauty and endless summer where no one ever dies again! I remember it all now!"

Procula searched the girl's face. "But there is more," she said in a moment. "And it seems even more significant in light of what you've just told me. You remember that I spoke of a lamb? Yes, well, a lamb is the *sacrifice* the Jews offer to *their* God at this Passover season! And I saw the lamb again near the end of my dream. Only this time the piercing eyes were in the face of the lamb. *The lamb had human eyes.*"

Livy gasped. She squeezed the lady's arm tightly. "But that's exactly what *I* saw!" she exclaimed. "That's what I was going to tell you! In the temple! On the altar . . . under the priest's knife . . . before the door of the inner sanctuary! There was a lamb—and it had human eyes!"

"The inner sanctuary? But how did you—?"

"I'm sorry, *Domina!* I know I wasn't supposed to look inside, but I just *had* to! In the middle of all that excitement—while everyone was so upset about Jesus turning over the tables of the moneychangers—that's when I—"

A knock at the door interrupted her. Melanus, the steward, entered in great haste, a pink flush glowing on the top of his shiny head, a grim look on his narrow face. Behind him the sound of a great turmoil could be heard in the street outside.

"My lady," he said, folding his long-fingered hands and bowing his bald head, "Master has asked me to escort you to the Tower of Antonia . . . for safety's sake. It appears that fighting has broken out in the streets."

CHAPTER 7

Livy quickly packed a few things in a bundle and followed Melanus and her mistress out of the room. A small detachment of five soldiers led them and a number of other servants and householders out of the palace. Then the small group turned northward and left the Upper City by way of a series of narrow streets and dark alleys. Their path followed the wall closely until it reached the city gate that led to the Skull Place—the Roman place of execution. From there it turned due east and took a winding course across Jerusalem to the Antonia, the tall, gray fortress whose battlements frowned down upon the temple enclosure from the northeast corner of the city.

Apparently the entire household was making this hasty move. Quintus was in the company. Cook, too. Even old Hatshup, bent as he was with arthritis and gout, was doing his best to keep up with the stiff pace set by the military men. At the head of the group Livy saw her master, Pontius Pilate, Prefect of Judea, conferring earnestly with the five Roman legionaries. She wondered what *his* feelings were about this emergency in the middle of the night.

As they hurried along, Livy heard the sounds of a desperate struggle behind them—angry shouts, hopeless screams, the clash of iron weapons. When she turned around she could see the flicker of flames lighting the walls of the buildings and wisps of white smoke floating in the moonlit air. The houses on either hand seemed to be huddling together in fear along the sides of the crooked, winding street.

Livy's heart began to pound in her chest as she surveyed this ominous scene. Though she couldn't see it, she knew what was happening. The revolution had come. The fight for freedom. She imagined the voice of the zealot speaking to her once again—*The time for action has arrived*. She pictured him in the thick of the fight, sword unsheathed, cloak thrown back, round head uncovered, teeth bared in a fierce expression of the joy he found in battling his enemies. That was how she remembered her father. *He* had looked exactly like that the very last time she saw him. And now at last—perhaps—she'd have a chance of seeing him again . . . when she was free. A wave of pride and self-satisfaction swept over her. With her help the zealot had made his decisive move! It wouldn't be long now!

Livy plodded along through the strange, silvery night, following Procula, Melanus, and the soldiers. But in her mind she stood once again in the kitchen facing the dark, gray-cloaked man. *If my friends and I succeed,* she remembered him saying, *you'll be free to go anywhere you want to go!* She wished she could be with him now, fighting the Romans at his side. She hoped he'd know where to look for her when the fighting was over.

As they passed the city gate, Livy glanced out into the darkness beyond the wall and caught a glimpse of Golgotha, the Skull Place. It looked eerie and lonely in the moonlight—a patch of bare rock streaked with the shadows of several posts fixed in the ground, like the gaunt trunks of dead, bare, branchless trees. She wondered what it would be like to be a condemned criminal—or runaway slave—heading out to that awful place to be crucified. *Not me!* she thought. *And not the zealot either!* For reasons she could not have explained, Livy had complete confidence in the man. Perhaps it was because of the self-confidence he exuded so profusely. She never doubted that his rebellion would succeed.

At last they reached the Antonia. Livy nudged Quintus and stared up at the massive stone walls that loomed above her head. Quintus frowned, bent his bushy head, and hugged himself. He looked as if he were tired and cold.

A guard on the tower shouted a challenge. One of the

soldiers replied with a password. This was followed by the creaking and grating of the heavy iron gates as they swung open to let the governor's party inside. Quintus cast a relieved glance behind him and shuffled forward into the safety and security of the fortress. Livy looked back toward the palace and the Upper City and wondered how the battle was going.

"Don't worry, my lady," said a smart-looking, square-jawed centurion, saluting the Lady Procula as she and her servant girl stepped within the fortification. "We've already beaten them. But it's best you stay here for the time being. There's no telling what they might try next."

Beaten! Livy stopped and stared at the man. With that one word her hopes and dreams of freedom—so bold and vibrant just moments before—crumbled into a heap of dust and ash. *The zealot and his friends? Beaten?* She felt as if a cold knife blade had suddenly pierced her lungs. Sucking in her breath, she shot a quick and silent glance at Quintus. Her coconspirator answered with a shrug and a confused grin.

"There weren't as many rebels as we had feared," continued the centurion. "Our men quickly gained control of the situation. Some of the zealots escaped. A few were arrested—those who survived the fight."

At this, the governor himself, wrapping his toga about his shoulders against the chill of the April night, approached the centurion. "What about the leader?" he asked, his balding head and eaglelike nose shining in the flickering light of the torches. "I've forgotten his name."

"He was taken, Excellency," answered the soldier. "In fact, he's here—in the fortress—awaiting trial before your tribunal in the morning. As for his true name, no one has been able to discover it. He calls himself Bar Abbas."

Bar Abbas! Livy started violently and searched the centurion's face.

"Bar Abbas—hmm, yes, that was it," mused Pilate, stroking his smooth-shaven jaw. "What kind of a name is that?"

"Aramaic. It means 'Son of his father.' Not really a name at all. We think it's a ruse—a way of protecting his family and friends. Either that or a code name of some kind. But we'll crack it."

"And the other one," continued Pilate, cocking an eye at the centurion. "What was his name? Jesus—the Nazarene. Did you arrest him as well?"

"No, Excellency. Apparently he wasn't involved."

There was a flurry of excited talk as the governor and his householders followed the soldiers down a long, echoing colonnade toward the commandant's quarters and the rooms they would be occupying during their stay in the Antonia. Livy walked along beside her mistress, holding tightly to her arm.

A predawn breeze wafted through the mosaic-tiled

corridor, which was open to a broad, flagstoned court-yard. It seemed to Livy that the fresh, fragrant spring air had grown unusually chill during their walk from the palace to the fortress. She felt cold inside, too. *Another chance—lost!* she thought. *But the zealot won't give up! He and his friends will try again! I know they will. They don't need this Bar Abbas!*

They rounded a corner. An adjoining passageway rang with the tread of heavy footsteps. Torchlight flared. Toward them strode two more Roman guards, a chained and darkly hooded prisoner between them.

"Well, well!" said the centurion, laying a hand on Pilate's arm. "Speak of the Devil! Here's your chance to ask him about it yourself, Excellency! Uncover your face before the prefect and his wife, dog!"

With a proud toss of his head the prisoner threw back his hood and faced them boldly. Livy choked back a gasp.

The round, close-cropped head; the long, snaking scar; the half-missing ear. There was no mistaking him.

She looked at him and he looked at her. Then he smiled—a bright, white smile behind thick black whiskers. With a swift and subtle motion he put one chained hand inside his cloak and lightly patted his belt. That was all.

"Get moving, Bar Abbas!" said one of the soldiers, giv-ing him a rough shove. "Your chamber's waiting! You'll have your chance to talk to the prefect in the morning!"

CHAPTER 8

Livy sat on a stone step before the entrance to the Antonia's prison, her chin in her hands. *What a night!* she thought.

She looked up and shielded her eyes against the glare of the late-morning sun. A figure was coming toward her across the flagstones of the courtyard. Its back was to the light, its face in shadow, and an explosion of wiry hair was flaming around its head like a halo—*just like one of the angels Cook is always talking about*, she thought.

But it wasn't an angel. It was Quintus.

"'Morning," said Quintus, rubbing his nose as he shuffled to a stop in front of her. "How are you?"

Just like he hasn't got a care in the world.

Tired as she was, Livy felt like getting up and punching him. "How am I?" she snarled. "How do you *think* I am?"

"I dunno. How am I supposed to know? Did you get any sleep?"

She scrunched up her nose and shook her red head at him. "This is no time to sleep! It's a time to be thinking, planning, doing! No, for your information—I didn't get any sleep! I've been up all night trying to figure out what we should do next. We've had a terrible setback, but we're not beaten yet! We need to put our heads together and get busy if we still want to win our freedom. Don't you understand that?"

The boy crossed his legs and scratched his left ear. "Sure I do. But things could be worse. At least there aren't any dogs around here."

She picked up a handful of gravel and threw it at him. "You're impossible!" she said.

Quintus ducked and retreated before the shower of small stones, his face buried in the crook of his elbow. "Stop it!" he cried. "I only came to tell you something!"

She glowered at him. "What?"

"Something I thought you'd want to know about. Mistress, too—especially her."

"Go on."

"Well, I was serving at Master's table early this morning when some men came in to see him—from the Jewish priests."

"And?"

"And they were talking about Jesus of Nazareth—the one we heard teaching in the temple yesterday."

"I know, I know. What about him?"

"They want Master to send soldiers to arrest him. They think he's dangerous. They're afraid—especially after last night—that he might, you know, pick up where Bar Abbas left off . . . get the people all riled up to fight the Romans or something."

Livy laughed. "*Him?* I don't think so!"

"Well, *they* do. They know where to catch him, too . . . after dark and away from the crowd."

Interesting, thought Livy. "So is Master gonna do it?"

"He said he'd loan them some troops from the fortress cohort. Tonight, after dark. I thought you should tell Mistress."

Livy squinted up at him. "You're right. She won't like it. She thinks an awful lot of this Jesus. Personally, I prefer a messiah like Bar Abbas. I think our chances were better with him." She paused and rubbed her chin thoughtfully. "Maybe they still are."

Quintus looked doubtful. "Whaddaya mean? He's in jail! He's no good to us now."

"Maybe. Maybe not. Besides, he's got incriminating evidence against me on his person . . . which makes me think I'd better stick with him as long as I can."

"But, Livy! He's a goner! Why, by this time tomorrow he'll probably be—you know—*chkkk!*" With his finger he made a slicing motion across his throat. "Why don't you just forget the whole thing?"

Livy cocked an eyebrow at him. "You give up too

easily, Quintus." She cupped one hand around her mouth, looked from side to side to make sure no one was listening, and whispered, "Bar Abbas may still have a few tricks up his sleeve. I've been talking to him about it."

"Talking to him! When?"

"This morning."

"You mean in *there?*" Quintus turned pale. His finger shook as he pointed down the dark stairway into the dungeon.

"Sure. Why not?"

"But—I didn't think the guards let anyone down there!"

"I have my ways," she said with a sly smile. "Want to see?"

"N-not really," said Quintus. But before he could utter another word, she had taken him by the arm and was leading him under the frowning archway and down toward the cells beneath the fortress.

At the first landing a rather sleepy looking soldier stumbled to his feet and barred their entrance with his spear. But in the next moment a look of recognition crossed his face and his features relaxed into a lopsided smile. "You again?" he said. "So what do you want now? And who's your friend?"

"Marius, this is Quintus," said Livy, bowing smartly as she presented the boy to the guard. "Quintus, Marius. Quintus is one of Governor Pilate's *personal* servants. In fact, he's just come from the governor's *personal* presence. To accompany me on an inspection tour of the prison facility."

Marius eyed Quintus with a skeptical grin. "Is that so?" he said.

"Livy!" whined Quintus, trying to free his arm from her iron grasp.

"Mm-hm," said Livy. "What do you say?"

Marius shook his head and mumbled something to himself, smiling all the while. He yawned and let out a loud burp. "I say anything's possible," he said with a wink. "*If* you can get me some more of that wine and cheese."

"There's plenty more where that came from," smiled Livy. "I'll be right back."

Quintus was obliged to wait with the soldier while Livy dashed off on her errand. Presently she returned with a bulging wineskin and a small goatskin bag filled with curdled white *leben*. She and Quintus left the guard happily eating, drinking, and muttering to himself. Then they proceeded down the stairway to the lowest level of the prison.

"Where did you get that stuff?" whispered Quintus as they wound their way down into the darkness.

"I told Cook that Mistress is waiting for her breakfast," Livy explained with an innocent look. "Which, of course, is true."

At the bottom of the stairs—a dank and murky spot lit only by the flame of a clay hand-lamp burning weakly in a shallow niche in the wall—Livy squeezed Quintus' arm and stopped in front of a thick wooden door bound with heavy iron straps.

"This is it," she hissed. She slid back a strip of iron that covered a narrow slot in the door and whispered through the opening: "Bar Abbas! It's me! I brought Quintus with me this time!"

Scraping, scuffling sounds reached their ears from the other side of the door. In a moment a single black eye, overarched by a bushy black eyebrow, appeared in the slot. A voice, harsh and gravelly but still recognizable, said, "Good. I've been working out a plan. And I have an assignment for you."

"An assignment," moaned Quintus. "Oh, no!"

The voice continued. "We've still got one chance left. Now listen carefully. You remember the agreement your master made with the Jews a few years ago? About releasing a prisoner of their choosing during the Passover festival each year?"

"That was right after the big uproar over the Roman military standards in the temple," said Livy. "He had to do *something* to restore his public image!"

"Right," said Bar Abbas. "Well, I intend to *be* that prisoner this year."

A slow smile spread across her face. Down in that

small space just beneath her heart Livy felt the dying embers of her dream—the dream of freedom—being fanned back into life. "*How?*" she asked.

"I have friends who can make it happen. They know the right people. They have contacts in every corner of the city, allies in almost every workshop and merchant's booth. I want you to go to them and tell them what I'm thinking. They'll have the word all over Jerusalem in less than an hour."

"You *really* think it will work?"

"There's a good chance. Anyway, we've got to try."

Livy glanced over at Quintus. He had dropped to the floor and was sitting with his head in his hands. "So where do we find these friends of yours?" she asked.

"Make your way back to the governor's palace and follow the street that goes past its main gate. Five houses beyond the palace of Caiaphas the High Priest you'll come to a house built of reddish stone. There's a mosaic in the pavement in front of the door—a picture of fishermen on the sea. You can't miss it. The house has an upper room that the owners rent out to visiting pilgrims. You'll find my friends on the lower level."

"And then what?"

Bar Abbas pulled a ring from his finger and passed it to her through the narrow slot in the door. "Give them this. Tell them what I told you. They'll know what to do. But you'd better go quickly. They may come and drag me before Pilate at any moment. And once he passes sentence on me, he won't wait long to carry it out."

Livy tucked the ring into her belt and grabbed Quintus' hand. "Got it!" she said. "Come on, Quintus— let's go!"

Quintus just shook his head and moaned.

CHAPTER 9

I t wasn't as easy to carry out Bar Abbas' assignment as
Livy had hoped. Although she wasn't sure how she and
Quintus would get beyond the fortress gate, she was con-
fident they could manage if given a chance. But Cook
kept them busy the rest of the day with kitchen chores.
And to make matters worse, try as they might, they just
couldn't seem to get away from Melanus. In all her six
years in Pilate's household Livy had never seen anything
like it. Most days, Melanus joined the other servants in
the kitchen for breakfast, handed out orders, then slipped
off somewhere by himself "to work on accounts." But
today he seemed to be everywhere, watching, checking,
threatening. Livy was sweating profusely before the day
was half over, more from anxiety than exertion.

It wasn't until the evening meal was finished and the
very last cooking pot had been scoured and stored away
that she thought she saw an opportunity to slip out.
Cook and Melanus were in another room, discussing the

state of household provisions. The sun was setting and most of the inhabitants of the fortress seemed to have gone indoors for the night. Outside, the city was unusually quiet, for this was the night on which many of the Jews celebrated the Passover meal with their families.

"Quintus!" she whispered as the boy came in with an empty water jar. "Get a cloak and meet me at the side entrance—you know, the small gate where they bring in supplies."

Quintus was about to respond, but she shoved him out the door. Then she ran to get her *pallium*, which she had left in the suite of rooms that had been reserved for Procula.

Maybe, she thought as she hurried along a vaulted passage—*just maybe—we won't ever have to come back! Maybe I can deliver Bar Abbas' message and then stay with his zealot friends! Then, once they've persuaded Master to release him, he'll come and smuggle me out of the city and I'll be on my way back to Gaul!*

She smiled to herself as she ducked inside the lady's chamber. Her *pallium* was there, draped across the ivory stool where Procula sat whenever Livy combed out her hair. She picked it up, threw it over her shoulder, and hurried to the door.

"Livia!" Livy turned to see her mistress coming in from another room. "I'm so glad you're here! I was just about to go looking for you. Come—sit beside me."

Livy's cheeks begin to burn. "*Domina!*" she faltered. "I was just—well, I—"

"Not now, child—please! I *must* talk to you! I—I have never felt so . . . so disturbed, so worried . . ."

Looking up at her mistress, Livy felt that it was true. Never had she seen Procula looking so worn and haggard. The skin of her face was extremely pale, almost transparent. Every bit of color had been drained from her lips and cheeks. "What is it, *Domina?*" she said, going up and laying a hand on her arm.

Procula dropped into an armchair of carved ebony. She motioned to Livy to sit on a scarlet cushion that lay on the floor beside it. Then, passing a hand over her eyes and sighing, she said, "After last night's trouble and our trek from the palace to the Antonia, I—well, I found it impossible to sleep. I paced this floor until well after sunup. Then, when my weary legs could no longer support me, I collapsed across my bed and fell asleep.

"I dreamed again, Livia! I saw the man with the piercing eyes—it was Jesus, I'm sure of it! He was carrying the lamb and he had a circlet of gold on his head. And this time he and the lamb went into the cage of fire! They were consumed by the flames! I wept and shouted, but I couldn't stop it from happening. What do you think it means?"

"I'm not sure," Livy said after a pause, her eyes fixed on the lady's face. "Back in Gaul, kings and chieftains wear golden circlets on their heads. The dream seems to be saying that the man with piercing eyes—Jesus—is a king. And a sacrifice, too."

"A king *and* a sacrifice?" It was clear that Procula was struggling to take it all in.

"Yes," said Livy slowly. "Whatever that means."

That was when it came back to her—the news Quintus had brought to her that morning outside the prison. The news he had wanted her to deliver to Procula. How could she have forgotten?

"*Domina!*" she said, jumping to her feet. "I just remembered something I was supposed to tell you! They're going to arrest him!"

"Arrest *Jesus?*" said Procula, taking the girl's two hands in her own. "Who's going to arrest him?"

"Master! And the Jewish priests! They're sending soldiers—tonight! Quintus heard them say so!"

Procula got up and crossed the room. She stopped in front of a small writing table. Taking up a stylus, she scratched a few words on a piece of parchment. She folded the parchment, sealed it with a spot of sealing wax, and pressed the insignia of her ring into the seal. Then she walked over and handed the parchment to Livy.

"You must follow the soldiers!" she said. "This letter will secure your passage out of the fortress. Take Quintus with you. Make sure the soldiers do not notice you.

When all is done, come back and tell me what you've seen. Now go!"

"Yes, *Domina!*" said Livy, taking the parchment from the lady's hand. Then she pulled her cloak up over her head and hurried out the door.

By the time she'd found Quintus it had dawned upon Livy that she was facing a nearly impossible task. She had accepted two difficult assignments: follow the soldiers on Procula's behalf *and* deliver Bar Abbas' message to his friends. And she had to complete both of them in a single evening. Already her palms were sweating and her heart beating as if it would jump out of her body.

Darkness was gathering as she and Quintus approached the soldier who stood on guard at the fortress gate. The man eyed them doubtfully as Livy pulled Procula's note from her pouchlike belt.

"*Seems* to be in order," he mumbled, studying the words on the parchment and chewing his lip thoughtfully. "Though I can't imagine why Lady Procula would send a pair like *you* two out into the streets after dark. What's this all about?"

"Ssshhh!" said Livy, pointing her freckled nose straight at the man's square chin and laying a finger to her lips. "It's top secret!"

The soldier frowned. Livy smiled back and gave him a wink. He cocked an eyebrow and glanced over at Quintus. Quintus just grinned and nodded.

Once outside the gate, Livy began to breathe a little more easily. *That part wasn't so hard*, she thought. She tugged at the boy's sleeve and pulled her own cloak up around her shoulders. "Let's get going!" she said.

Her companion scratched his bushy head with nervous fingers. "What for?" he whined. "*I'm* in no rush to land myself in a big heap of trouble!"

Instead of answering, Livy took him firmly by the arm and dragged him after her over the uneven paving stones. She knew there wasn't a moment to lose.

Following Bar Abbas' instructions to the letter, they hurried west to the gate that stood opposite the Skull Place, then south along the wall to the old Upper City. It wasn't long before they were passing the gates to the grand old Herodian palace, the governor's normal residence in Jerusalem. Its massive stonework towered above them imposingly. Except for a few sentries who had been posted at the entrance, the place was deserted—dark, empty, and silent. As she rushed past, Livy couldn't help wondering whether she would ever return to the palace. She hoped not. If only Bar Abbas' plan might work! There was still a chance that her days as a slave were nearly over.

A few blocks south of the palace and on the opposite

side of the street stood the rich-looking, Greek-columned structure that served as home to the high priest, Caiaphas, and as an occasional meeting place for the Sanhedrin, the Jewish Supreme Court. Livy recognized it at once.

"Five houses beyond . . ." She repeated the words of Bar Abbas to herself as she and Quintus rushed ahead. "One . . . two . . . three," she counted, ". . . four—I think this is it, Quintus! Reddish stone . . . mosaic in the pavement . . . upper story . . . yes, this has to be it!"

For a few moments they stood hesitating, staring first at the fishing scene pictured in the tiles at their feet, then at the low-arched door before them. Then came a sound from above their heads. They looked up. The door to the upper room had opened, and a group of plainly dressed, dark-bearded Jewish men were coming down the stairway. At their head was a tall man with a familiar face. A face Livy had seen before. A face with dark brown eyes that seemed to pierce her very soul. She put a hand to her mouth and caught her breath.

It was *him!* Jesus of Nazareth.

Slowly, Jesus and his men descended the stairs. When he reached the bottom, he paused momentarily and turned to look at Livy. It was a sad look, she thought. Without intending to, she gripped Quintus' arm more tightly and backed away. Something caught in her throat. In that small space beneath her heart she felt something fluttering like a dry leaf in the wind. Why was he here? What would she say to him if he spoke to her? What would he think if he knew what she was doing? *Did* he know? How could he?

But the Galilean did not speak. Instead, he turned and led his followers up the street. Dumbstruck, Livy and Quintus watched them go. In a few moments they had rounded a corner and were heading up a street that led to the eastern portion of the city.

Livy let out her breath with a small sigh as the last of them disappeared. "Let's go!" she said. "It's getting late— I can feel it."

"What do you mean 'late'?" asked Quintus. But Livy didn't answer. She was already at the door of the red-stone house, pounding on it loudly with her fist. She waited, then knocked again. The door began to open, slowly, very slowly, just a crack. Around its rough wooden edge appeared the dirty fingers of a hardened hand. From the darkness within, two shining eyes peered out. A low voice spoke: "Who's there?"

By way of answer, Livy reached into her belt and drew out Bar Abbas' ring. Its gold surface glinted dully in the night air. She thrust it into the crack between the door and the frame. The callused hand seized the ring eagerly and drew it inside. Then the door closed.

Livy turned and looked at Quintus. Quintus frowned. "Is that it?" he said. "Can we leave now?"

"Leave! We haven't even delivered the message yet!"

She was about to knock again when the door re-opened and the hand beckoned them inside. Quintus turned on his heel, but Livy grabbed him by the tail of his cloak and pulled him in after her. Once behind the closed door, she found herself looking up at the owner of the two bright, beady eyes she had seen staring at her through the crack in the door. They were burning under bushy eyebrows, set deep within a large-nosed, terribly scarred, gray-bearded face. The face leered at her frighteningly in the light of a handheld lamp.

"Where did you get this?" said the man, holding up Bar Abbas' ring. It glittered in the yellow lamplight. There was a musty smell in the house, like the stench of something rotten. Livy thought she heard drunken shouts coming from an inner room. She let go of Quintus, planted her feet firmly beneath her, and swallowed.

"It's from Bar Abbas!" she blurted out in a voice that seemed too high and thin to be her own. The tiny inward trembling had grown so strong that it was shaking her entire body. "He gave it to me—in the Antonia prison."

"Then he lives!" breathed the man, nodding his head and examining the ring closely in the lamplight. He turned his face toward her. "What's his message?"

Livy smoothed down her cloak and tunic and cleared her throat, searching for her voice. When she thought she had found it, she answered, "He says the governor will release a prisoner for the Passover. He says he wants to be that prisoner. He says . . . well, he said you'd know what to do."

The man regarded her with a strange, toothless smile. "Of course we do," he said. "When's his trial?"

"He's already been tried! And condemned!"

"Then we'll have to work fast," he muttered. He held the lamp above his head and kicked the door open. "Now you'd better make yourselves scarce—fast!" With that, he thrust the two children out into the street. Quintus collapsed on the pavement with a sigh of relief. Livy stumbled over him.

"Wait!" she called. "Bar Abbas and I made a deal! He said that when he's released, he'll—"

The door slammed shut. Livy and Quintus were alone in the darkening street. She shook herself, picked herself up, pushed her hair out of her eyes, and turned to give Quintus a hand.

"Well," she said shakily, "I guess that's that. Come on—we'd better get back to the fortress as fast as we can! I just hope those soldiers haven't left yet!"

CHAPTER 11

There's no point in going back inside," she whispered to Quintus when they found themselves standing once again in the black shadow of the Antonia. "I don't want to have to convince that guard that Mistress Procula is sending me out on *another* top-secret errand!"

Quintus nodded. "I don't even want to *go* on any more top-secret errands," he said.

Livy ignored the comment. "We'll just stay right here," she said, leading him close to the wall, "in the shadows—until we see the soldiers of the cohort. I just hope we're not too late."

They didn't have long to wait. Soon the sound of voices reached them from somewhere within the darkened archway. This was followed by the scraping and grating of the heavy iron gates swinging open and the heavy tramp of the soldiers' feet as they marched out of the fortress. Livy and Quintus flattened themselves against the wall to keep out of the light of the torches. It was hard to be sure in the darkness, but Livy guessed there must be at least 200 of them.

"A whole army to arrest one man?" she wondered out loud as they passed. "I don't believe this!"

Once beyond the gate, the cohort turned left and began moving in the direction of the temple. Livy and Quintus followed cautiously at a distance.

"What're they going in there for?" whispered Quintus as the troops made another left turn into the temple grounds.

Livy didn't answer. Instead, she grabbed his hand and followed the soldiers.

"What's this?" she said when they emerged inside the Court of the Gentiles. "*More* soldiers?"

It was true. Across the open square marched a smaller detachment of temple guards in their brass helmets, white turbans, and blue tunics. Some were armed with clubs and spears. Others carried torches and lanterns.

"Dogs!" said Quintus when he saw them, turning pale and ducking behind Livy. "Oh, no! Livy, you don't expect me to face all those dogs, do you? I couldn't do that for *anything!* Not for Mistress Procula or freedom or Bar Abbas or—"

"Quiet!" she hissed. "They're all on leashes! Besides, they're after Jesus, not us!"

As Quintus settled into a soft whimper, Livy stared

narrowly at the man who walked at the head of the troop of temple guards. She was almost certain she had seen him before . . . that very night . . . on the stairway descending from the upper room. Yes! That was it! He was one of the men who had been with Jesus! One of his friends!

What does it mean? she wondered. *Has he come to beg the* soldiers *to leave his teacher alone?* But there was no time to grope for answers. Already the combined Roman and Jewish forces, their armor and weapons glittering in the torchlight, were leaving Jerusalem by way of the Golden Gate and marching down into the Kidron Valley.

"Come on, Quintus!" she said. "We've got to keep up with them!"

But Quintus wasn't the only one who was having trouble matching the soldiers' pace. Livy, too, was struggling against the onset of a terrible weariness. She'd had very little sleep over the last two days. The state of constant mental and emotional confusion in which she had been living since the beginning of the week was taking its toll. To make things worse, the path became much harder for the two young slaves from this point forward. The importance of remaining unseen obliged them to hang back, beyond the range of the torches and lanterns, and in the thick darkness it was extremely difficult to pick their way down the valley's steep and rocky side. They stumbled, tripped, and fell several times before reaching the brook. Their attempts to get across the water left them soaked and muddy. By the time they were across the brook, they had lost sight of the soldiers altogether. Livy's heart sank. What would she tell her mistress?

Stumbling up the other side of the valley, Livy felt her inward thoughts and resolutions beginning to break apart. *Why are we even doing this?* she wondered. Conflicting images passed before her mind's eye: Procula's pale, distraught face; the black eye of Bar Abbas peering through the slot in the prison cell door. Swords flashing in a desperate fight for freedom; piercing, sad eyes turned upon her at the bottom of the stairs. A lamb under the priest's knife; a basket of fire; a man with a circlet of gold upon his head. What did it all mean? What was the point? And what did she care about this man Jesus, anyway? What could Bar Abbas do for her now that he was in prison facing execution? She didn't want to think about either of them. All she wanted was her freedom!

So tired was Livy that Quintus had actually moved ahead of her as they continued their climb up the slope beyond the brook. Vaguely, through the darkness, she saw the boy approaching a line of dark brush—almost like a hedge—at the top of the rise. A sudden thought struck her. She stopped and called out to him, "Quintus! Wait! I've got a better idea!"

Quintus turned and stood squinting down at her as

she ran to catch up with him. By the time she reached his side, she was fighting to get her breath.

"What better idea?" Quintus asked.

"Don't you see?" she said when she was able to speak at last. "We're outside the city! Outside the walls! This is what we've been waiting for!"

Quintus scratched his head. "It is?"

"Take a look around! There's nobody out here! It's dark! This is our chance to make a break for it! We don't need anybody else's help—we can be free! We *are* free!"

Quintus was backing away, staring at her as if he couldn't comprehend what she was saying. "But what about the soldiers? And Mistress Procula? And Jesus of Nazareth? And Bar Abbas?"

"Forget about them!" said Livy. "Let's just go for it!"

At that moment, from somewhere in the surrounding darkness, a chorus of loud barking broke in upon their discussion. Quintus turned white. His bottom lip began to tremble.

"I knew it!" he moaned. "It's those dogs, Livy! They're here! They're gonna get me!" He turned to run, but tripped over a tree root and went crashing through the tangled hedge in front of them.

"No!" cried Livy. "Don't do this to me *now!*" She plunged after him into the bushes.

To her great surprise, she emerged in the midst of what looked like a neatly kept garden. White roses, yellow chrysanthemums, and pink coriander bloomed in well-watered beds. Ferns lined stone-paved paths that went winding away into the night. Twisted olive trees gently bent their limbs over the entire scene.

Quintus was lying on his back beside her, a dazed, uncomprehending look on his face. Looking up, she became aware that the place was blazing with light. Torches were flaring. Dogs were barking. Angry voices were shouting. Suddenly Livy realized that the soldiers and temple guards they had been following were in the garden too. But to her great relief she also concluded that none of them had seen her. Their eyes were directed elsewhere—at someone who was standing at the other side of the garden. In a glare of light and a confused hubbub of noise they pressed toward that person, weapons drawn, shields at the ready.

"That's the one!" someone was shouting. "The one Iscariot just kissed on the cheek! Seize him!"

"Betrayed with a kiss!" laughed another harsh voice. "That's a good one!"

Fear caught at Livy's throat. *Betrayed? Caught?* Who were they talking about? She looked wildly from side to side but was unable to see anything clearly.

Suddenly there came a lull in the noise and the confusion. A gap opened in the crowd. Livy looked up and saw him—Jesus of Nazareth—standing in the midst of the guards and soldiers, a serene, self-possessed expression on his face.

"Whom are you seeking?" she heard him call as several armed temple guards approached him.

"Jesus of Nazareth," they responded.

"I am He," answered Jesus, fixing them with his piercing eyes.

At that moment something very odd happened. It was, in fact, the strangest, most wonderful thing Livy had ever seen. As she watched, those deep, clear eyes began to glow with an unearthly light. They shone—or so it seemed to her—like pale stars in the heaven of Jesus' plain, humble face. Livy rubbed her own eyes and stared. Could it be true? Was the night air around Jesus' head and face shimmering like the air above the desert sands on a hot, summer day? Had his beard actually changed from brown to snowy white? Had a tongue of flame really shot across the space between him and the guards as he spoke those three simple words, "I am He"? Livy didn't know what to think, what to believe.

But whatever it was that she saw, the soldiers seemed to have seen it too. Their faces went colorless with terror. The muscles in their arms and legs went slack. Some cried out, some whimpered, some moved their lips soundlessly. Dropping their weapons, they all stumbled backward and fell to the ground before the Nazarene's gaze. Jesus stood looking down at them, waiting, it seemed, for them to speak.

"Wow!" said Quintus, sitting up and gaping. "Did you see that?"

"I—I think so," said Livy. Her eyes were as round as two coins. Her mouth hung open. *Maybe I was wrong about this man*, she was thinking. *He does have a gentle, plain-looking face, but*— Her thoughts ceased in mid-sentence. There were no words in her vocabulary, no space in her brain for a man who could do the kind of thing she'd just witnessed. Only the gods could look and speak like that.

When the men, looking stunned and embarrassed, had risen to their feet and brushed themselves off, Jesus put his question to them a second time: "Whom are you seeking?"

Timidly, picking up their weapons and retreating a step or two, the soldiers answered him again. "Jesus of Nazareth."

"I have told you that I am He," said the man with the piercing eyes. His voice was calm and quiet, but inside Livy's head it sounded like thunder. "Therefore, if you seek Me, let these go their way."

At this the barking and shouting broke out afresh. The soldiers rushed forward, seized Jesus with rough hands, and bound him with a rope. In the next moment both his voice and his face were swallowed up in the crowd. Livy grabbed Quintus and pulled him back into the safety of the bushes as several men—followers of Jesus, apparently—went running this way and that. Then the soldiers and their dogs moved off, leading Jesus out of the garden and down the hill. The light of their lanterns faded into the quiet distance. Livy and Quintus found themselves left alone.

"Now what?" said Quintus, rubbing his head. "Are you serious about trying to escape? I'd hate to have those dogs on *my* trail!"

Livy frowned into the darkness and watched the glow of the torches as they retreated into the valley. Her brain was a blank. The small space beneath her heart was numb. She wasn't quite sure what she had just seen. She *couldn't* be sure until she'd gone home and had a good night's sleep. Yes, that was it. She was overtired—completely exhausted. First she'd rest. Then she'd have to think the whole thing over for a while. Of one thing she was certain: she had misjudged this man Jesus. He didn't look like much on the outside, it was true. But it was obvious that he had some kind of terrible power within him. She had to know more about him. She couldn't run away without finding answers to the questions that were burning in her mind. She bit her lip and chewed the inside of her cheek. Then she brushed the red hair out of her eyes and turned to face Quintus.

"No," she said. "I've changed my mind. We're going back."

CHAPTER 12

Livy woke with a start in the predawn darkness. Her eyes popped open at the sound of a cock crowing in the black emptiness outside the window. Something in the bird's voice—so raw and shrill in the early morning air—chilled her. She sat up shivering and pulled her linen tunic on over her head.

At once the events of the previous night flooded back into her mind. The house of Bar Abbas' friends . . . Jesus on the stairs . . . the soldiers with their torches and lanterns . . . the hike across the Kidron Valley and up the Mount of Olives . . . the arrest of Jesus.

Arrested. Jesus had been arrested! Jesus—a man who could knock down a troop of soldiers with a mere glance! *That* was a picture that would remain etched in Livy's memory for a long, long time. Never had she seen any man, in Gaul, Rome, or Palestine, who possessed that kind of power. Maybe Cook was right. Maybe this Jesus *was* the Jews' long-awaited Messiah after all—the

Liberator, the Deliverer . . . the one who would set *everyone* free. But if so, why had he allowed the temple guards to bind him and lead him away?

Then it occurred to her that her mission was still unfulfilled. She hadn't yet given her mistress a report on last night's events! She had to find Procula at once and let her know what had happened in the garden on the hill outside the city. Livy got up, threw her *pallium* around her shoulders, and ran down to the kitchen.

Cook was there, wrapped in a blue-and-white shawl, brooding silently over a steaming pot. A fire blazed on the great stone hearth. There was a delicious smell of barley broth and baking loaves in the air. The big woman looked up slowly as Livy came running in at the door. Her eyes said it all. *She knows.*

"Where have they taken him?" Livy blurted out. "Do you know? Can you tell me?"

Cook's eyes grew round with surprise. She obviously hadn't expected the slave girl to be so concerned about the Nazarene's arrest. "Caiaphas' house, so far as I can tell," she said, shaking her head sadly. "Leastwise I haven't heard anything about them bringing him *here*. Master's up, but he's still at his breakfast. I'm not sure what he's got on the docket for today."

"Livy!" said Quintus, shuffling in behind her. "There you are! I've been looking all over for you. I've got news I thought you'd want to hear."

"What is it?" she asked. "Is it something about Jesus?"

Like Cook, Quintus seemed taken aback at the urgency in Livy's voice. "Well, yes . . . as a matter of fact, it *is* about Jesus."

"What? Tell me!" she demanded, grabbing him by the sleeve.

"Leggo of me, wouldja?" said Quintus. He backed away and smoothed the wrinkles out of his tunic. "He's going to stand trial before Master," he said. "Right away. I heard it while serving at table this morning. Messengers from the chief priests were just here."

"Here?" said Livy. "They're bringing him *here*?" Even she was a bit startled at the tone she was taking. Why this churning feeling in her stomach? Why this feeling that something *had* to be done?

"Isn't that what I just said?"

"It was bound to happen this way," observed Cook, still shaking her head. "And I have a feeling it'll lead to no good. You mark my words."

A trial before Master Pilate! thought Livy. *Maybe there's something Mistress Procula can do to help!*

"Cook!" she said. "Have you seen the Lady Procula this morning?"

"Not yet, child," said Cook, turning back to her pot. "Probably still in bed. She's hardly ever up this early.

Can't blame her, either—doesn't sleep well with all those dreams and such."

Livy didn't wait to hear any more. She was out the door at once, crossing the flagstones, heading toward the stairs that led to Procula's apartment on the second level of the fortress. But as she crossed the courtyard, she saw something that caught her attention and made her stop for a closer look. In front of the open space before the governor's quarters—at the judgment place known as *Gabbatha*, or the pavement—a crowd of Jewish priests and officials was gathering. *They're here—already!* she thought. *And Jesus must be with them! Master will be coming out to speak with them any minute!* Her mistress would want to know about this development at once.

Again she ran, passing beneath an archway, through a series of columns, and around a dark corner. The stairs lay straight ahead. But when she reached the bottom step, she stopped and stared. There on the first landing stood a tall, dark figure, awaiting her approach and blocking her path.

It was Melanus.

"Well, well," smiled the balding steward in his most soothing, melodious voice, "if it isn't the very person I've been looking for!"

"You've been looking for *me?*" said Livy, scrunching up her nose and scowling. "What for?"

"It's actually rather interesting," he responded, calmly

folding his long-fingered hands. "The captain of the dungeon guards came looking for me last night—in my capacity as overseer of the household slaves, you understand. He asked about you specifically. Apparently there's a prisoner down below—a condemned man—who wants to see you."

Bar Abbas! thought Livy. In the midst of all the excitement about Jesus' arrest she had forgotten about him! He, too, was expecting a report from her!

Melanus unclasped his hands and took a step toward her. "Is it possible that Lady Procula's *personal servant* is really acquainted with rebels and criminals of that sort?" he continued with a thin-lipped smile. "It's hard to imagine! Definitely not the kind of information one wants to get around. You'd have been wiser to keep the thing hushed up. Perhaps it's time you and I had a little talk." He reached the bottom of the steps and stretched a hand out toward her. Livy swerved, dodged, and ran back the way she'd come.

Tearing back across the courtyard, she again passed the place of judgment, where the governor was addressing the small crowd that had gathered before his tribunal bench. Quintus was standing behind him and off to one side; apparently he had been assigned to attend to his master during the course of the trial.

"What accusation do you bring against this man?"

she heard Pilate say as she hurried toward the entrance to the prison.

"If he were not an evildoer," someone answered, "we would not have brought him to you . . ."

No chance of seeing Mistress Procula now, thought Livy. *Not until Melanus is out of the way.* She looked up and saw the dark stone archway that led to the dungeon on her left. *This may be my only chance to talk to Bar Abbas,* she thought, ducking into its shadow. *But I'd better make it quick!*

She hesitated only a moment. Then she hurtled down the steps, past the dozing guard, all the way to the lowest level of the prison. There she stopped, breathing heavily, and leaned for a moment against the cool stone wall of the passageway. Sliding the strip of iron away from the peephole, she pounded heavily on Bar Abbas' door. "It's me!" she said.

The dark eye quickly appeared at the opening. Livy thought she detected a glint of fear in its expression. "Finally!" said the voice from within. "What took so long!"

"No time to explain," she answered breathlessly. "I can't stay—Melanus is after me! But I delivered your message—just the way you told me. Any news here?"

"Yes," was Bar Abbas' somber reply. "They brought me before Pilate yesterday afternoon. The long and short of it is, I'm scheduled to die today. Crucifixion. Myself and another poor wretch they took on the night of the uprising." She could not mistake the note of despair in his voice.

There was a pause. "I'm sorry," Livy said at length. *I wonder what he's done with my parchment*, she thought. *I wonder if they searched him when they brought him to trial.* She tried to ignore the sinking feeling in the pit of her stomach. "But—well, you just can't give up hope!" she went on. "Not now! Your friends are spreading the word this very minute! I—I'm sure they'll fix everything so that you're the one released for the festival. And then . . . and then . . ."

She stopped. *And then what?* Livy had to admit that she didn't know. What about Jesus? What about Procula's dream? Was she *really* hoping for Bar Abbas' release? Should the guilty go free while the innocent are punished? And who was the true liberator? The zealot or the Nazarene? She wasn't sure. She no longer knew what she wanted. And she didn't have time to figure it out now.

"I-I've got to go now," she stammered. "Melanus is sure to find me here if I stay another second! There's another trial going on. I'll keep you posted if I can."

"Another trial?" she heard him say as she jumped back up the stairs. But she didn't dare stay to answer. She still had to see her mistress, and there wasn't a moment to lose.

For the third time Livy crossed the courtyard. As she

passed the tribunal, she saw Jesus standing before Pilate. Despite her fear of being caught, she felt she had to stop and listen.

"*Are* you the King of the Jews?" she heard her master say, his voice echoing over the paving stones and off the fortress walls.

"Are you speaking for yourself about this," Jesus replied, "or did others tell you this concerning Me?"

King of the Jews? Livy thought of the Lady Procula's dream . . . of the man with the piercing eyes, crowned with a circlet of gold. Could it be that this Jesus really *was* a king? Was the governor simply mocking him? Or did he really want to know?

From across the open plaza came a sudden, unmistakable glint of light—the reflection of the rising sun off the top of a shiny bald head. Melanus had seen her and was moving determinedly in her direction. She turned and ran.

Through the colonnade, around the corner, and up the staircase she flew. She reached the door of her mistress's chamber and beat upon it loudly.

"Who's there?" came the lady's worn and weary voice from behind the door.

"Livia!" she answered. The steward's sandals echoed on the stairs behind her. "Please, *Domina!* Let me in!"

The door flew open and Livy slipped inside. She fell

into her mistress's arms and clung to her. "Lock it!" she pleaded. "Quickly!"

The lady did so, giving her servant girl a worried look. The sound of footsteps passed and faded in the passage outside. Livy breathed a sigh of relief.

"What is it?" said Procula in an alarmed voice.

"They've taken him!" she said. "Arrested him—Jesus! He's on trial this very minute—before Master's tribunal! I don't know what they might do to him, but Cook says it won't be good!"

Procula said nothing. Her mouth hardened into a firm, straight line. The creases in her forehead, only half hidden by her curls, bunched together. Then, as Livy ceased speaking, the fear and anxiety that had dominated her features melted away and were replaced by a look of determination. She stepped to her writing table, took up a stylus, scribbled a note, and sealed it. When she was finished, she recrossed the room and handed the parchment to her servant.

"Deliver this message to Pilate," she said. "Immediately."

Livy's face brightened. Perhaps the lady's note would save the Galilean's life! "Yes, *Domina!*" she said. Without a moment's hesitation she thrust the door open and burst out into the passage.

Down the stairs she raced and across the Antonia's broad middle courtyard. She never stopped until she had climbed the 10 steps to the tribunal.

Quintus glanced over at her as she crossed the platform. He frowned and mouthed the words, "What are *you* doing here?" In reply, Livy merely put a finger to her lips and held up the parchment. Then she stepped straight up to the governor.

The eyes of Jesus gripped and held her as she drew near. Mesmerized for the moment, she stopped and stared. Then she heard him speak, apparently in answer to another one of Pilate's questions. "My kingdom is not of this world," he said. "If My kingdom were of this world, My servants would fight, so that I should not be delivered to the Jews; but now My kingdom is not from here."

"Are you a king, then?" said Pilate, stroking his smooth-shaven jaw. He smiled—a doubtful smile. Then, as if coming out of a reverie, he suddenly turned and saw Livy standing at his side.

"What is this?" he said with a scowl. "Who authorized this interruption?"

"Begging your pardon, Excellency," said Livy in the sweetest and most timid voice she could manage, "but my lady, your wife, Mistress Procula, has sent me to you with a message." She held the parchment out to him.

Pilate's eyebrows arched upward. "From my wife?" He frowned. "Very well, then. Give it here."

As inconspicuously as possible, Livy sidled up next to

him and peered over his toga-clad arm as he unfolded and read the note. It said:

Have nothing to do with that just man. I have suffered many things today in a dream because of him.

"A dream," sighed Pilate. "Yes, and what else is new?" Then he turned to the servant girl and said, "Tell your mistress that her message has been delivered. That will be all."

"Yes, *Domine*," said Livy.

With that she hurried away from the pavement. She still wasn't sure why she was so concerned about this Galilean teacher. Perhaps it had something to do with the things she had seen in the garden the night before. Whatever the reason, she returned to her mistress's chamber feeling that she had done everything in her power to help him.

CHAPTER 13

Livy spent most of the remainder of the morning in her mistress's room, trying to sort out her feelings about the events of the past two days. It was odd. Now that the excitement was over and the waiting had begun, she couldn't help feeling as if a dark cloud were hanging over her head. There was a kind of numbness in that small space just beneath her heart—as if she were just too tired to care about anything anymore. She sat on the little ivory stool with her chin in her hands. Procula noticed her silence.

"You, too, are troubled," said the lady, glancing over at her servant girl with a look of deep concern.

Livy looked up and tried to smile. "I'm just thinking," she said.

Procula herself found it impossible to restrain the flow of her words. Livy had never seen her so highly agitated. She worried aloud about the outcome of the Nazarene's trial. She paced the room, talking nervously, referring constantly to her dream and the strange pictures it contained. She couldn't stop thinking, she said, about Livy's explanation of those symbols. There were so many unanswered questions. How could Jesus be *both* a king *and* an innocent victim? She did not understand it, though she was convinced that it must somehow be true. Nor could she bear to think that her own husband might be the cause of his innocent suffering. She hoped that Pilate would heed her message and let the prisoner go.

Livy, too, could not stand to think that the teacher from Nazareth might become the innocent victim of Roman abuse. She didn't want to think about suffering. Hadn't there been enough suffering already? She wanted to get *away* from suffering. She wanted to go back home to Gaul. Not the real Gaul, but the Gaul of the Otherworld. The land she had seen in her dreams. That place where sunlight gleamed on the blue sea-waves and flowers bloomed all year, where there was no slavery, pain, or death, but only brightness and unending joy.

What good can suffering—and dying—possibly do anyway? she thought. *How can that set anybody free?* She thought back to the first time she had seen Jesus, a whip in his hand, a righteous fire in his eyes. She wondered why he didn't rise up and drive Pilate and the priests away as he had the merchants and moneychangers in the temple. She began to doubt that he was the Messiah. Who needed a suffering Messiah? Maybe she should have changed her mistress's note to read: *Pilate: You must release the prisoner Bar Abbas at all costs. Signed, Procula.* She squeezed her eyes shut, shook her head, and sighed. *What a crazy idea!* she thought.

Then it dawned on her. She was angry. Yes, *angry.* Why had she allowed this thing to get her down? True, as a Celt, she had inherited her people's natural tendency to melancholy. But she was also an energetic, fiery, high-spirited young girl. She was not used to feeling depressed. She had to break this pattern somehow. She had to get out of this stuffy room and find something to do—anything at all—to help her forget about Jesus and Bar Abbas and liberators and messiahs and slavery and freedom and the whole sorry mess. She stood up and walked to the door.

"Livia! Where are you going?" said her mistress as she laid her hand on the latch.

"I'm sorry, *Domina.* I've just got to get out for a while. Maybe I can . . . find out what's happening and let you know. I'll be back soon."

Out in the corridor, she found a back stairway that did not lead to the open courtyard. She darted down the steps, taking them two at a time. Then she directed her course to the northwest corner of the fortress, away from the center of the action, to the gate that led through the city wall and out toward the hills north of Jerusalem.

This portal opened onto a drawbridge that crossed a

narrow, rectangular body of water known as the Stru-thion Pool. The bridge could be pulled up during a siege, but was usually left down. There were iron gates at both ends of the wooden span—the outer one locked and guarded by a sentry, the inner kept open except under threat of invasion.

This is perfect, thought Livy. She bent down, picked up a handful of loose gravel from the base of the fortress wall, and strode out onto the bridge. There she sat down, dangling her feet over the dark water, and began drop-ping pebbles into the pool. As near as she could figure, it was already past noon—the sixth hour of the day.

What had come over her during the past week? Sure, she wanted her freedom. But what good was freedom if you were too dull and serious-minded to enjoy it? She had allowed things to go too far. What had become of the old Livy—the prankster, the joker? Somehow, she had to get back to being her fun-loving self!

Choosing a small rock, she reached back and heaved it toward the outer gate. It struck the iron bars with a tiny *clang!* The soldier on guard peered in through the grating and scowled at her. Livy smiled puckishly, shrugged her shoulders, and gave her dangling feet a little kick.

But what was this? As Livy watched, another shape appeared beside the soldier outside the gate, a shape Livy wasn't looking for and hadn't expected to see again—

ever. The dark shape of Kalb, the big black dog. As he caught sight of her, the dog's big feathery tail began to wag back and forth. He whined and gave a short, friendly bark.

What in the world— thought Livy.

The sentry prodded the dog with the butt of his spear. "Off with you, mutt!" he growled. But Kalb refused to move. Livy had a strong feeling that he was not looking at her, but had fixed his eyes on something beyond her, at the other end of the bridge. His tongue was hanging out, and his tail was lashing happily from side to side.

That was when her attention was distracted by another sound—the sound of a voice that came from behind her back.

"Livy!" called the voice. "I've been looking all over for you!"

Quintus. *What's he doing here?* she wondered. *Isn't he supposed to be waiting upon Master at the trial?* She turned and saw him approaching.

Then it struck her. *Quintus . . . the dog . . . the old joke! This is just what I've been looking for! Just the thing to get me out of the doldrums!*

In a flash she was on her feet and calling to the soldier at the gate. "Oh, thank you, sir! I'm so glad you've found him!"

The man looked confused. "Found who?" he said.

"My dog!" Livy answered, reaching through the bars

to stroke Kalb's black head. "I thought he was lost for good!"

"*Your* dog?"

"Actually he belongs to my mistress—the Lady Procula."

"The Lady Procula?"

"Yes! Could you please open the gate and let him in? Oh, she'll be *so* happy to see him!"

The guard frowned. "Well, I suppose I'll have to if he really belongs to the governor's wife."

No sooner was the gate unlocked and opened than Kalb bounded inside with a joyous bark—just as Quintus set foot on the other end of the bridge. With a happy yelp the big animal shot past Livy and lunged at the boy, catching him completely off guard. Livy saw the look of surprise in Quintus' eyes. She held her breath and restrained her laughter, waiting for his cry of terror.

It never came. Instead of screaming, turning, and running, Quintus came straight on, waving his arms over his bushy head and shouting, "Livy, I've got something to tell you! Something important!"

Before he could say another word, the dog was upon him and the two of them were tumbling over the edge of the bridge and into the Struthion Pool.

Looking down into the water, Livy saw Quintus' head come bobbing to the surface. She watched as he coughed and spluttered. She was waiting for just the right moment to laugh in his face. But when he opened his eyes, she saw something in them that stopped her cold. They held no fear of the dog. In fact, it was clear that Quintus wasn't thinking about Kalb at all. Whatever his message was, it had possessed him entirely and he was bursting to deliver it. He opened his mouth and let it out.

"Livy!" he shouted. "They let Bar Abbas go! They're going to crucify Jesus!"

CHAPTER 14

Let Bar Abbas go?

That was Livy's first thought. It tumbled quickly through her mind as Quintus struggled to keep his head above the water. *Bar Abbas free? So his plan really worked! And that means . . .*

"Couldja help me out of here, Livy?" spluttered Quintus, flailing an ineffectual arm in her direction.

It means I've got to find him somehow!

"Livy!"

Her second thought, which came tearing in from the other side of her brain with enough force to shatter the first, was, *Crucify Jesus? The gentle, humble teacher? The man with the piercing eyes? No! It can't be!* Why the sudden, empty ache in the space beneath her heart?

"Please, Livy! I can't swim!"

She knelt and gave Quintus her hand. "Crucify?" she said, pulling him to a sitting position on the edge of the bridge. "But *why?* What did he do? Bar Abbas tried to lead an armed revolt! He killed people! *Jesus* didn't do anything like that!"

Quintus sat there shivering and pushing his dripping locks out of his eyes. Kalb scrambled out of the water beside him and shook his black body from head to tail, soaking both children with a shower of spray. "As far as I could tell," said the boy, reaching up to scratch the top of his head, "the only thing they had against him was that he's some kind of king. King of the Jews. I didn't know it was a crime to be a king."

A king! Livy remembered the words she had heard Jesus speak as he stood before Pilate at the place of judgment: "My kingdom is not of this world . . ." *Of what world then?* Could he be king of the *Otherworld?* And if king of the Otherworld, wouldn't he also be—well, some kind of a *god?* Of course! That would explain what she had seen in the garden!

Through her mind raced images from her mistress's visions and pictures of the Otherworld as she had heard it described in the tales of her Celtic homeland. She recalled her own dream: the sea and the sky; the familiar faces wreathed in smiles; flowers piled in great heaps up to the heavens. *The Otherworld. King of the Otherworld.*

"I don't understand it," Quintus was saying. "I mean, nobody punishes me for being a slave. Master's the governor, and that's all right for him. If Jesus is a king, then let him be king. What's wrong with that?"

But Livy wasn't listening. Her thoughts were intent upon yet another mental picture: three upright posts in the rocky ground, gaunt, still, black, and silent in the moonlight outside the city gate. *The Skull Place! That must be where they've gone*, she thought.

Suddenly the full significance of the situation struck her with a sense of sickening horror. She, Livy, had helped Bar Abbas' friends secure his release. And because Bar Abbas had gone free, Jesus, the king of the Otherworld, was going to the Skull Place to die! *No!* she thought. *This can't be happening!*

"Come on, Quintus!" she said, grabbing him by the sleeve of his soggy tunic. "We've got to follow them! We've got to stop them somehow—or at least try!"

With a single yank she hauled her bewildered companion to his feet and pulled him along after her. Then the two of them, followed by the great black dog, tore across the bridge, through the inner gate, down the echoing corridors of the fortress, and out the main entrance. When the guard challenged her, Livy simply flashed him the note her mistress had given her the night before. It was enough to keep him from asking any further questions.

From the Antonia they followed the winding city streets that she knew would lead them across Jerusalem and out to Golgotha, the Place of the Skull—the Romans' place of execution. They could see at once that a large crowd of people had recently passed that way. Bits of broken pottery and various personal possessions—a head scarf here, a leather pouch there—lay scattered across the ground, apparently dropped by onlookers as they followed the procession of the condemned. Most telling of all, Livy thought she saw spots of blood on the uneven paving stones—blood from the backs of the prisoners, who would have been severely beaten with whips just before being led out to the place of crucifixion. A few stragglers were hanging behind and talking in hushed tones about the executions Pilate had ordered for the eve of Passover Sabbath. Convinced that she was on the right track, Livy pushed on.

She followed the foreboding trail over the cobbled surface of the narrow streets, beneath dark arches, through the shadows of the crowding houses. The sky had grown dark—strangely dark, she thought—darker than she had ever seen it in the middle of the day. Kalb and Quintus followed closely at her heels as she turned left, then right, then left again, panting with exertion, until the wall and the Western Gate appeared before them. There she stopped.

Through the gate Livy could see the gathered crowd. In spite of the darkness, she dimly caught a glint of dull light from the helmets of the soldiers assigned to the execution detail. She heard the chatter of the casual observers, the rough laughter of the rabble, the harsh shouts of the legionaries. Here and there arose the cry of a child or a woman's muffled groan.

Above this scene, atop a rise of rocky ground, she saw the three upright posts. To the posts had been attached three heavy wooden crossbeams. And hanging from the crossbeams were the anguished forms of three dying men. Livy sucked in her breath and put her hand to her mouth. At this distance it was impossible to see the faces clearly, but somehow she knew. The one in the middle was Jesus of Nazareth.

"We can't stop here," she said to Quintus, who stood beside her, pale and dripping with perspiration. "Let's see if we can get any closer."

"Why is it so dark?" said Quintus as they passed beneath the arched gate and began to climb the rocky hill of Golgotha. Through the dusky air Livy could see the terror in his eyes. "Cook said no good would come of this! What do you think is happening?"

"I don't know," she answered softly. She was racking her brain for details from the old stories her mother used to tell her back in Gaul. Could the King of the Otherworld—a god himself—possibly die? And if he did, would everything else die with him? Was that the reason for the darkness? Was the whole world coming to an end?

"We shouldn't have come, Livy," Quintus was moaning. "What're we gonna do *now?*"

"I think I might be able to suggest something," said a deep voice at their side. Startled, Livy turned to face the speaker.

Through the darkness a row of white teeth emerged from beneath a black moustache. The contours of a round, closely cropped head took shape against the sky. Kalb let out a happy bark and leaped toward the dark, stocky figure. A thrill of mingled fear, hope, and doubt jumped within her.

"Bar Abbas!" she said.

It was indeed Bar Abbas. She saw him reach into his belt, pull something from it, and hold it out to her. "I believe this belongs to you," he said. "I no longer have any need of it."

"The parchment!" she gasped. She snatched it from his hand and quickly shoved it into her belt. "Then it's true!" she stammered. "You've been set free!"

"Yes. And I've come to free you, too!" he said.

"But where are you going?"

"Oh, I don't know," he said, waving his hand carelessly. "Far away from here for the time being—to Damascus, maybe. With my friends. Long enough for things to settle down. We'll take you along if you like. From Damascus you can get passage to Asia Minor, and then to Greece, Macedonia, and Gaul. What do you say?"

Slowly, Livy drew the piece of parchment out of her

belt and peered at it through the gloom. The words scrawled upon its surface struck her now as a series of harsh, mocking questions—*Bar Abbas? Freedom fighters? Messiah? Liberator? King?*—questions for which she still hadn't found any satisfactory answers.

A chill came over her. She shivered and shook herself. This was the moment she'd been waiting for, wasn't it? *Freedom.* It lay within her grasp at last! So why didn't she feel happy? Why wasn't she excited? Why this churning, gnawing feeling in the pit of her stomach?

"I don't know, Bar Abbas," she said, looking up at him. "I—"

She stopped. There was a hand on her shoulder. A hand with a firm, pinching grip. A narrow, long-fingered hand.

"So!" said a calm, self-satisfied voice behind her. "Still consorting with criminals, I see. Is the Lady Procula aware of your choice of friends?"

"Let go of me, Melanus!" said Livy, wrenching herself from his grasp.

Bar Abbas stepped forward and planted a finger on the steward's chest. "Correction," he said with a smile. "A *pardoned* criminal."

Melanus looked up with a sour smile and pushed the zealot's hand away with the back of his wrist. "Apparently so," he said with a tone of distaste. "But *your* good fortune has little bearing upon *my* responsibility as head steward of the governor's household—which, at the moment, is to return these two *escaped slaves* to their master. *If* you will excuse me."

Bar Abbas looked at Livy. Livy looked at Quintus. Quintus shook his head and moaned. Kalb bared his teeth and growled.

Suddenly a loud volley of thunder set both earth and sky trembling. The ground began to shake violently. A cry of dismay went up from the crowd. Some of the people turned and started running back to the city.

"Oh, no!" groaned Quintus. "Oh, no! We're all gonna die!"

Then came a rumble like the sound of stampeding elephants as, without warning, a deep fissure opened in the earth at their feet. Melanus leaped backward with a shriek, narrowly avoiding a fatal tumble into the widening crack. "The day is accursed!" he shouted. Then he took to his heels as more large cracks opened in the ground around them. Rocks and boulders came rolling down the hillside, scattering the frightened spectators in every direction.

Quintus stared, wide-eyed. Kalb barked and wagged his tail. Livy put a hand to her forehead and swallowed hard.

"Let's go!" shouted Bar Abbas, taking Livy by the hand. "I'm not sure what's happening, but we'll *never* get another chance like this!"

But Livy pulled away. She set her jaw and looked him in the eye. "No!" she shouted.

Bar Abbas' forehead wrinkled. "What do you mean, *no?*" he said. "We're going! Leaving! Escaping! You're on your way to freedom! Isn't that what you want?"

Slowly, the quaking of the earth ebbed and stopped. A chilling rain began to fall. Livy sat down on a rock and put her head in her hands. She felt hot tears welling up in her eyes. "I *did* want it," she said, glancing up at the zealot. "But now I'm not so sure."

"Not sure!" said Bar Abbas, his face turning red. "Why not? What are you talking about?"

Livy stared straight into his eyes. "It's all wrong!" she said. "I *can't* leave now. Not until I know what's going to happen to *him.*" Through the rain and the dispersing crowd she pointed to the top of the rocky hill, where the Nazarene and two other men hung dying on Roman crosses.

"*Him?*" said the exasperated Bar Abbas. "I can tell you what's going to happen to *him!* He's going to die—if he's not dead already! Now, are you coming or not?"

"No," Livy said in a trembling voice. "Don't you see? It's because of *me* he's hanging there! It's because I helped *you* gain your release instead of him! And I was wrong! It should never have happened this way! But now that it has, I—well, I've just got to see how it all turns out. Mistress Procula will want to know." She buried her face in her arms.

Bar Abbas pulled his gray hood up over his head. "Have it your way, then," he said. He whistled to his dog. Kalb whined and licked Quintus' hand.

"I won't forget what you've done for me," added Bar Abbas. Then, without another word, he turned on his heel and strode off into the pouring rain.

————

It was a long time before Livy became aware that the rain had stopped—hours, maybe. She really had no idea. She felt empty, depleted, terribly quiet inside—like the night sky after a violent storm has passed. When she looked up at last, she saw that Quintus was sitting on the ground beside her. He smiled at her weakly, but said nothing.

Livy turned her eyes toward the top of the hill. Everyone had gone home. The crosses were empty. Ragged clouds were drifting off to the east. The late afternoon sun was sinking toward the sea.

"We'd better get back, Quintus," she said, getting to her feet. "*Domina* will be wondering what's become of us."

CHAPTER 15

No one knew what to make of Melanus' disappearance. Though Pilate's men searched the city and made diligent inquiries in all the surrounding villages, no trace of the steward was ever found. The servants, of course, all had their pet theories. Livy's was that he had fallen into one of the huge cracks that opened in the earth during the quake on the afternoon of the crucifixion. Quintus thought that sheer terror must have driven him crazy and caused him to run away. Cook believed that heaven had struck him because of his proud and blasphemous statements about the Messiah. It was the talk of the household all the following day—an excited buzz that ran from the servants' quarters to the kitchen and out into the courtyards and stables.

But on the third day—the first day of the week—there was something else to talk about.

It all began at breakfast. The threat of further rebellion being past, the governor's household had moved back to the old Herodian palace, and the servants had gathered in the kitchen for a share of Cook's broth and bread. Hatshup, the Egyptian gardener, was squatting in his accustomed spot near the oven, hunched over a bowl of broth, chewing his bread with gusto and enthusiastically nodding his old gray head.

"I'd gone down there very early to dig up a few lilies and anemones," he was saying. "Master Joseph's gardener had promised me some—for that bed out near the fountain. It needs a bit of brightening up. The crocuses were a disappointment this year, and—"

"We don't care about your old crocuses!" Cook cut in, turning fiercely from her pot. Her upper arm jiggled as she shook her ladle in his face. "We want to know exactly what you saw!"

"Yes, Hatshup," said Livy. "Please tell us." She drew her stylus and writing tablet from her belt, ready to catch anything that might be worth jotting down.

Hatshup's bony frame shook with silent laughter. He grinned from ear to ear. "I wish you could have seen the looks on those guards' faces!" he said. "Like they'd seen a ghost! Maybe they were *expecting* to see one—or something even more terrible—at any minute. I don't know. But I *do* know that the stone had been rolled away. I saw that much myself! And they had no idea how it happened! Doesn't take much to put one over on *them*, I guess!" He bobbed his head and grinned.

"Wait a minute!" said Livy, looking up from her tablet. "You're saying that the big stone had been rolled away from the entrance to the tomb? Why? Did somebody try to steal the body?"

"Don't know," said Hatshup, swallowing. "Couldn't stay to find out. Had to get those lilies transplanted before they started to wilt."

Quintus whistled. "But it would take at least 10 men to budge a stone that size!"

Hatshup raised his eyebrows, nodded, and slurped his broth noisily from a wooden spoon.

Livy bent over her tablet, pushed her red hair away from her face, and wrote: *Sunday morning. The tomb of Jesus. Stone rolled away. Don't know why.*

She couldn't wait to tell her mistress. Once her own breakfast was finished, she quickly prepared Procula's and hurried with it up to the lady's room. But no sooner had she stepped inside the door than Procula began pouring forth some exciting news of her own.

"I've had another dream, Livia! Please come in—set the tray down. Another dream! But so different this time! I don't know when I've slept so well or so deeply. And in the deepest part of my sleep I saw myself on a hillside covered with flowers. The colors were brighter, more intense, more *real* than anything I've ever known! Not dreamlike at all. It was as if the world had been created all over again. And Jesus of Nazareth was there, coming down the slope toward me. He was dressed all in white, with the golden circlet on his head. And behind him came a great crowd of people from every nation on earth—like the crowd we saw that day in the Court of the Gentiles! He came to me and took my hand. Then I joined the others and together we walked toward the sunrise." She paused, her eyebrows compressed in thought. "Since Jesus of Nazareth is dead, what can it mean?"

"I'm not sure," said Livy, setting the tray of food on a carved and polished table of acacia wood beside the lady's bed. "But I've got something to tell you, too! Old Hatshup was in that garden early this morning—the garden near the tomb where they laid his body—and . . ."

There was a knock at the door and Quintus came bursting in. "Livy! Mistress Procula!" he said. "I thought you'd want to know! I was serving at Master's table when some soldiers came to see him. They looked really worried. They said that the garden tomb wasn't just open. It was *empty!*"

Livy and Procula looked at one another. "And what do they take it to mean, Quintus?" the lady asked.

"They don't know," said Quintus, hitching up his tunic. "But I heard that some of his followers—Jesus' followers, I mean—are already saying that he's alive again! Risen from the dead! One of them says she saw him walking around in the garden!"

Procula turned to Livy, a hopeful light shining from her eyes. "What do you think?" she said.

Livy chewed her lip. "I think," she answered slowly, "that if the king of the Otherworld *could* die, he would only do it if he knew it would help the rest of us somehow. And I think that, when it was all over, he'd *have* to come back . . . like the morning sun and the flowers in spring. My mother told me a story like that once, when I was very little—about a king who went on a journey to the land of the dead, and suffered many things for his people, and then returned to them again. I also think," she continued, "that if he *could* conquer death and if he *did* come back, then maybe he'd—well, *forgive* us . . . for everything!"

Procula said nothing, but simply watched the girl with a curious look of anticipation on her face.

"Most of all," Livy concluded, "I think we'd better go and find out if all this is true."

"My feelings exactly," agreed her mistress, reaching for her cloak and throwing it over her shoulders. Then she glanced from Livy to Quintus and frowned. "But how?"

"We could try to find some of his followers and ask *them*," suggested Quintus.

"Good idea. But do you know *where* to look?"

"Yes!" said Livy, a tingle of excitement running

down her spine. "I *do* know! The house down the street! The red-stone house with the fishing mosaic in front. The one with the upper room! Maybe they're still staying there!"

"All right, then," said Procula. "Let's not waste another minute."

"I'll lead the way!" said Quintus, almost tripping over his own feet in his haste to get out the door.

Livy was about to follow him over the threshold when Procula laid a hand on her arm.

"Just a moment, Livia," she said. Then she bent her head and took off the fine gold chain she always wore around her neck. "I want you to have this."

"*Me?*" Livy looked up into the lady's eyes, a warm but uncomprehending glow growing in that small space beneath her heart. "But why, *Domina?*"

"As a token of my gratitude—for helping me find what I believe will be the path to a new life," said Procula. She smiled, then added, "*And* as a symbol of your newfound freedom."

Livy blinked and wrinkled her freckled nose. "My— *freedom?*"

"Yes."

Livy shook herself. "You mean . . . when I come of age—right?"

"No. I mean today. Right now. As of this very minute. And if you're willing—if you freely choose it—I'd also like to make you my daughter. I will ask Pilate to help me arrange the adoption as soon as we return from our investigation. What do you say to that?"

For a moment Livy didn't know *what* to say. She felt as if her heart had jumped into her throat. Procula saw her hesitating and laid a hand on her shoulder. "I understand if you'd rather not give me your answer right away," she said. "I know how you've always cherished the hope of finding your real parents again someday. If you'd rather think it over and . . ."

"No," said Livy, looking up into her face. "It's not like that. There's a place in my heart where I've always felt that—that I'd never see them again until we all get to the Otherworld . . . that maybe they didn't survive the raid and the battle after all. I don't know. What I *do* know is that you've been like a mother to me all these years, and—well, I don't think they'd blame me for loving *you*, too. Do you?"

There were tears in Procula's eyes. "Of course not," she said. "And what's to stop us from searching for them together?"

"Nothing!" said Livy with a sudden burst of joyous energy. She hugged her mistress and buried her face in the folds of her long white *stola*. At last she blurted, "In that case, I don't need to think it over. My answer is *yes!*"

Then, hand in hand, they went out together—the

slender, graceful woman and the tall, red-haired girl. For Livy, it was the end and the beginning. The end of the life of slavery. The beginning of the freedom she had fought so hard to gain.

But I never thought it would happen this *way*, she thought as they stepped out into the bright April air. *Not even in my wildest dreams!*

Letters From Our Readers

Who was Bar Abbas, anyway?

Brendan Jones, St. Paul, MN

The Bible doesn't say a lot about Bar Abbas, also known as Barabbas. We just know he was a zealot who was involved in a plot to overthrow the government, and that he was the prisoner chosen for release during the Passover. Bar Abbas is mentioned in Matthew 27:15–26, Mark 15:6–15, Luke 23:18–19, and John 18:40.

Wasn't it dangerous for Livy to trust and help a man like Bar Abbas?

Holly McCord, Newark, NJ

Yes! Your parents have, no doubt, warned you about trusting strangers—and Bar Abbas was a stranger *and* a criminal. But sometimes people do unwise things. Livy had been kidnapped and taken away from her home and her people at a very young age. Her longing to see her family overcame her natural fear of this rough stranger.

Livy didn't know the whole story about Bar Abbas, either. She saw him as a man who was willing to fight for freedom—someone who could help her escape. She didn't know he was a murderer. Once she recognized the consequences of helping Bar Abbas—that she'd unwittingly played a part in Jesus' crucifixion—she realized how mistaken she'd been in helping him.

Did Pilate's wife really dream about Jesus?

Annie Britt Poole, Oshkosh, Wisconsin

Yes, she did. In Matthew 27:19, the Bible tells us that Pilate's wife, who was not a Christian at the time, asked her husband to release Jesus because of a dream she'd had. God has often used dreams to give special messages to people, both believers and nonbelievers. Check out these examples: Jacob (Genesis 28:10–17); Joseph, son of Jacob (Genesis 37:1–11; Genesis 40—41); King Nebuchadnezzar (Daniel 4); Joseph, husband of Mary (Matthew 1:20; 2:13).

However, we must not assume that our dreams will come true or that they are special messages from God.

Who were the "Celts"? How could their strange religious beliefs possibly help Livy understand who Jesus was?

Tristan Firth, Waukegan, Illinois

The *Celts*, called "Gauls" by the Romans, were a group of people who in ancient times inhabited parts of France, Spain, Britain, Ireland, and Asia Minor. They were the ancestors of today's Irish, Welsh, Bretons, and Scots. The Celts were *pagans* who believed in many false gods and practiced many strange religious rites—including human sacrifice.

The Bible tells us that *all* the world's people—even unbelievers who have never heard of Jesus—have an empty space in their hearts that only the true God can fill. They may not realize it, but everyone is searching for *Him* (see Ecclesiastes 3:11; Acts 17:24–31; Romans 2:14–15). Their desire to know God sometimes shows up in odd ways in the religious beliefs they invent for themselves. For example, the Celts believed in the need for human sacrifice. That concept was very close to the Christian concept of a sacrificial Savior, but the Celtic method of finding favor with their gods—killing innocent people—was wrong. Only God could provide a sacrifice for our sins. But because Livy was familiar with the *concept* of an innocent person as sacrifice, she recognized Jesus as the Savior and Sacrifice her people had been looking for all along—without even knowing it!